TO HAVE AND TO HOLD, TO LOVE AND TO KILL:
AN AGREEMENT OF SOULS

I0582594

AMY S. CUTLER

Black Rose Writing | Texas

Author photo taken by Victor Coreas of Focus Media

Copy editing done by Anne-Marie Rutella

ISBN: 978-1-68513-342-9
PUBLISHED BY BLACK ROSE WRITING
www.blackrosewriting.com

Printed in the United States of America
Suggested Retail Price (SRP) $19.95

To Have and to Hold, to Love and to Kill: An Agreement of Souls is printed in Gentium Book Basic

*As a planet-friendly publisher, Black Rose Writing does its best to eliminate unnecessary waste to reduce paper usage and energy costs, while never compromising the reading experience. As a result, the final word count vs. page count may not meet common expectations.

This book is dedicated to Christine, who taught me that there is, perhaps, an entirely different explanation for our struggles.

To every soul that my soul has been led to find comfort with, and to the one that has become my guiding light, thank you.

TO HAVE AND TO HOLD, TO LOVE AND TO KILL:

AN AGREEMENT OF SOULS

1
THE ACCIDENT

The vodka bottle bounced around the car as it flipped once, twice, three times. It hit the roof and settled there, the car upside down, windshield shattered, blood mixing with broken glass and sunlight to turn the interior a slight shade of red. The bottle, it turns out, was the only thing in the car left unbroken.

Each seat was crumbled with the frame of the Jetta, the upholstery torn from the toss, the glass, and the landing. The radio was dead, broken from the inside out. Julie was dead, also broken from the inside out, heart stopped thanks to the pressure of the steering wheel she was pressed against, lungs burst, her rag-dolled body cocooned by the wreckage.

Outside, one sneaker lay next to a brand-new Schwinn bicycle. The bright blue Ked matched the color of the bike, both a birthday gift from that very morning. Eight-year-old Kenny never knew what hit him as he carefully rode to school that morning, sticking to the sidewalk like his mother had instructed, being a big boy for the first time ever. In his mind, he kept replaying the conversation that happened as he was slurping up the rest of his Apple Jacks.

"Please, Mommy, I love my new bike so much and wouldn't it be fun if I got to show it to Billy and Kate?" Kenny had always dreamed of riding by himself to his elementary school. "It's just one and one-half blocks, Mommy, and you can even watch me until I turn the corner."

Kenny's mom knew this day would come—she even facilitated it by buying the bike—but she would always worry. He was her baby, her only child since her husband had died shortly after he was born. She would have wrapped him in bubble wrap if she could.

"Plleeaaasseeeeeee," he begged, wrapping his skinny arms around her, whispering in her ear, "I promise to stay safe."

Vicky gave in, as she almost always did. She may have been overprotective, but she was also a pushover. "Okay," she told him, squeezing his tiny frame. "But you have to promise to be a big boy and stay on the sidewalk."

At first glance, anyone at the scene wouldn't have even seen Kenny, tossed into the bushes next to Mr. Chaney's house, inches from the street. He died with a smile on his face, not even having time to change his reaction from joy to surprise to agony to death, the best birthday gift that he received being the gift of unawareness. His mother was also unaware, as he had already turned the corner and had only eight houses to pass before he reached the schoolyard. She had decided to give him some space and count to thirty before walking down their street to peek around the corner. As she walked the block to the corner, Vicky put her face to the sky and soaked in the sunshine, proud that she was finally getting some of the vitamin D that her doctor had insisted she get.

Moments before Vicky reached the end of the road, she waved at Mrs. Viola, Kenny's favorite teacher *on the entire planet*, as her son would say. Mrs. Viola didn't even seem to see her, as she took the corner too fast, her sky-blue Jetta squealing as she made the turn. Seconds later, a dull crunch rang in the air and Vicky thought that the teacher had hit a tree. She sped up to make sure that Mrs. Viola didn't need help.

Julietta Viola, Julie for short, realized just as she was passing one of the moms that she recognized from conferences that she had an almost empty bottle of vodka sitting in her cup holder. She mistook it for her coffee. Grabbing it, she turned for the briefest of seconds to stash it on the floor behind her, under an umbrella. Her head ached and she blinked as she sat back up straight, getting slightly dizzy and pressing on the gas by accident. Almost missing the turn, Julie slammed on her brakes and lost control of the car for only a fraction of a second. Time slowed as she saw a boy, too late, riding a bicycle.

She jerked the wheel hard to the left, but it didn't matter because she had already plowed Kenny over as if he was a twig or a bag of trash. That's what it felt like to Julie, but the impact must have been greater because as the bike flew up over the windshield, the car flipped in the other direction, tumbling a few times, and coming to rest on its roof, with one final crunch.

Rounding the corner, Vicky saw these things at the same time: the wrecked and upside-down car, one bright blue Ked, a brand-new but crumbled Schwinn bicycle, and what seemed like an entire street full of blood. Stunned, Vicky scanned the scene for her son, and her eyes landed on his feet sticking out of Mr. Chaney's bushes. No time to breathe or think, she ran to him, checking for a nonexistent pulse.

"Somebody please help us," she sobbed, choking as shock set in.

She heard footsteps running toward them, saw hands gently pulling her son out of the bushes and onto the concrete where CPR could be done. Mr. Chaney was holding Kenny's head and neck still while another man she didn't recognize tried to breathe life into her lifeless child. To Vicky it felt like she was watching this unfold through a haze, as if she were being pulled under a wave and could not fight her way back to shore. Her son was already dead, she felt it right in her belly, the same place that always pulled at her when she absolutely knew that he needed her.

Vicky turned, in slow motion, to see the rescue crew attempting to pull Mrs. Viola from the wrecked car. Rage filled her entire being as she was torn between watching people unsuccessfully bring her child back to life and attacking the person who did this to him. She half walked, half crawled over to the paramedics who were struggling to free Julie's body. She pushed right past them and, on her knees, grabbed the dead woman's face and screamed. It was all of Julie that she could grab, her body still sandwiched between the steering wheel and the seat, upside down and sticky with blood. Vicky had to be pulled from Julie's body, cutting herself on the broken glass and metal of the car, not caring about anything except rage, because rage is always better than sorrow.

2
THE PROMISE

Julie watched this scene unfold from...well, from everywhere. At the moment of impact her body died and full awareness set in. *Oh no, no no no no no no no. What have I done? Oh, Kenny. Oh no.*

She had killed someone, a child, and even worse one of her very own students. And why? Because of booze. Because she was weak and lonely and forgot that the very reason she had even been alive this time around was to help people. Julie looked on as Vicky, wrapped in a blanket that one of the paramedics had put on her, knelt beside her dead son and sobbed. She was alone now, with no way of knowing that in just a few short weeks, she would be given a diagnosis that would allow her to be with her son and husband again.

A bright white light broke the scene in two, like a lightning strike only brighter, and Julie witnessed little Kenny's departure from this life. One moment, he was lying on the ground, chest being pumped by tiring hands, and the next he was standing above his body, holding hands with a man who looked just like him, only older. His dad. Kenny whispered, "I'll see you soon, Mommy," into his mother's ear before the man lifted Kenny into his arms and began to walk away. After just a few steps, Kenny scrambled from his father and ran back to where his mom knelt on the ground. He whispered again, but this time Julie could not understand what he said. Kenny ran back to his father and was again lifted into his arms. Incredibly, the boy, still with just one blue sneaker on, turned to look at Julie, holding eye contact until he was almost out of sight. A slight smile played on his lips as he waved goodbye.

Another crack in the sky and that same light appeared for Julie. She turned her back to it, ashamed of how her life had played out. She couldn't accept such a welcoming light, not this time.

"Jules," a soft voice tickled her ear. "It's time," the voice said, clearer now as a man appeared at her side. James, the love of her life, the love of so many of her lives. Her soul mate.

Julie sank closer to Earth, away from James, away from the warmth of the light. "This is wrong," she told him, crystal tears running down her face. "This wasn't supposed to happen. That boy had more life to live. I killed him." This moment was usually a happy one, the rejoining of souls, a celebration. Not this time, not this life. Julie felt like all was lost.

"You can't plan for everything, my love. All you can do with the time given in life is your best," James tried to continue but she wouldn't hear it. She didn't care about human nature and free will, about mistakes and forgiveness. In all her lives, she had never killed someone, would never have agreed to that.

"I missed you so much when you died. I did not remember that we would be together again. It felt like the sun had stopped rising, as if I were living in a constant state of darkness. I was lost, but still, I had no right. I have to pay for what I have done." Julie finally turned to James and let him hold her.

"Twenty-five years, eight months, sixteen days, four hours, and thirty-two seconds. In human terms, about a quarter of a life. That is how long I have been waiting for you to come home to me." James kissed the top of her head. "Please just come, rest, and try again. You *can* still help people. There is always time."

She pulled away, shaking her head and watching the light begin to fade. "I cannot come with you. I don't deserve the rest, or the forgiveness."

The energy started to swirl around them as James fought for the right words. Pinks and greens dipped and swirled over the scene, and as the emergency services crew zipped up Kenny's body, even they noticed the colors. "We have had hard times before. The Catholic persecution in Britain? I was lynched for harboring a Catholic—you—before you killed yourself to escape torture. We lost three children to the Spanish flu, their bodies left in the street while we suffered our own fates. Or the time when you were a spy for Washington and were caught by me? Only I did not know you and I turned you in, to find out after death that I had sentenced my own soul mate? Is that not as bad as the life of one child, who will certainly grow to greatness in his next life?"

Julie shook her head, the sadness rolling off her in waves of gray, and took his hand. "You know the difference between predestiny and an accident," she reminded him. "I can't just move on. Not until you promise me that I will pay for this. This must be set right. I cannot ask that boy's soul to return, to waste a life just to punish me. Please." Julie was quietly begging, and James knew what he would have to do, quickly, before the light was gone and they were lost.

He held her hand up, putting his palm against hers. "I promise, in our next life together, we will be apart. You will know sadness. And when the time is right, I will bring your death."

Julie almost smiled. "And I will be scared? And I will suffer?" Right then, to Julie, punishment was the most important lesson of all.

"It is my promise to you. You are my soul mate, and I will do anything to bring you peace, even if that means killing you."

Julie didn't even have time to consider what James was giving up for her. Their hands glowed in the light that came rushing into them, the promise sealed for eternity. No time to reconsider, Julie leaned into James, but he was instantly torn from her. Both of their souls tumbled toward the light, and both entered the world again. Together but completely alone.

3
THE LONELIEST EXISTENCE

Twenty-five years, eight months, sixteen days, four hours, and thirty-two seconds. A quarter of a lifetime, and the exact amount of time that, long ago, Julie lived without James in her life. Also, the exact amount of time before Nicole Ingles, or Nikki, as her small handful of acquaintances called her, hit rock bottom.

Some people hit rock bottom when they are strung out on drugs. Others when the alcohol gets the best of them, or abuse finally breaks their spirit. For Nikki, it was all those things, wrapped into one. In her words, when she finally dared to speak them, her entire life was a *complete shitstorm*.

Nikki took a breath as she surveyed the small room of people. Some of them looked pretty high still, but the majority were clean and sobor, many clutching on to their sobriety chips. "Hey everyone, my name is Nikki, and I guess I'm supposed to tell you how I came to be here," Nikki addressed the room but kept her eyes locked on the crumb-covered linoleum floor. She wasn't ready to tell her story, but she wanted that one-month chip, and part of the process was sharing. That's what her sponsor told her anyway.

"Hi, Nikki," the room chanted back.

It made her even more uncomfortable, everyone knowing her name. She should have given them a fake name, like Susie or Barbara, a nice, normal-sounding name, but it was too late. She noticed the swirl of the single fan in the room blowing the crumbs around.

"So, a few months ago, I was fired from my temp job at the Broad Hill Mall department store, the one down between the old arcade and the Dollar Store. I don't know why they call it a mall, seeing as how there are only a handful of stores in the strip, and they don't even have fancy names. Just department store, hardware, toys, stuff like that." She was rambling and had to rein herself in.

"Anyway, I was fired. I had been fired from the past three temp jobs and the so-called agency that I got work through told me that I had run out of chances. Nancy, the receptionist, basically hung up on the last call, telling me that I had better grow up and get serious before all the pretty was beaten out of me. I was fairly sure that Nancy should have been the one getting fired, but there was nothing I could do. It wasn't my fault that my boss thought that private work meetings meant feeling his employees' private parts. Apparently, he had never heard the word *no* before. The next morning, I got a call from the agency that I had been fired for insubordination."

Now, Nikki knew, came the hard part. She clasped her hands together, nervously, and said, "I am actually kind of proud of the fact that I got fired for something that wasn't my fault, because the other times were definitely my fault. I did what I had always promised myself I would never do, and I became an addict. That's what got me fired. I would use my shitty life as an excuse to get drunk or high, but really, getting drunk or high didn't help me out of my shitty life. I've been fired for falling asleep while waiting for fries to cook. I've been fired for shoplifting the clothing that I was refolding in the bargain bins. I've been fired for showing up late, not showing up at all, and showing up stoned out of my mind. The job with the handsy boss? That was the first job that I shouldn't have been fired for—well fired for *yet*, since I *was* planning on borrowing a little advance out of the register."

Breathing out. Breathing in. Nikki went on, "Anyway, after that I was out of work and money, so I hooked up with a pimp who had been trying to recruit me for a little while. I did all right at first, since the twits who wanted to touch me this time around were paying for it, not to mention the drugs that came in a steady stream. I was earning a living off the creeps who supplied me with a fix whenever I needed it, until Nancy's prediction came true, and someone finally did beat the pretty out of me." Nikki unclasped her hands and put one to the side of her head, where her stitches were still healing. "I didn't even know what happened at first. One minute, I was slowly rolling down my black fishnet stockings, dancing to the beat of Billy Joel's 'My Life,' thinking that the guy I had met up with that evening was pretty cute. I started to have this stupid little fantasy about being swept away like Julia Roberts in *Pretty Woman* when an ash dropped from the cigarette between my lips and landed on the rug. The *hotel's rug*, not even my date's own personal rug, when the guy flipped out and picked up one of my heels and smashed me in the face with it before screaming that I was a dirty whore who should live on the streets, all the while kicking me and insulting everything from my slut mother to my unborn demon children."

Nikki wiped a tear from her eye as she managed to get the courage to look around the room. She was surprised that they didn't look bored, and the faces that had all seemed so uncaring at the start of her little confession suddenly looked friendly, as if there was now some secret between them and it would maybe bring them together.

She continued, making eye contact with her sponsor as she finished her story. "Strung out, mostly naked with only one half of a torn fishnet intact, and insanely thirsty, I was left, broken and bleeding, in the hotel's parking garage dumpster. I was thrown away like a piece of trash, which I figured was the message. The thing was, I felt like trash and so it seemed like a perfectly reasonable place for me to spend the night. And in the morning is when Ken found me, sleeping in the dumpster with a trash bag covering my battered body like a blanket. I imagine I gave him quite a shock, but he never showed me anything but absolute kindness. I went from living the loneliest existence to having a caring brother-type friend. Ken dusted me off and helped me out when I felt completely hopeless. He helped me see that I am an addict. That was tough, since I had always blamed any drinking or drug issues on circumstance, and here was some guy telling me that I can change. Then he brought me here, to all of you, and for that I am grateful." Tears were running down her face now, but she smiled and gratefully accepted her shiny red coin. "Thirty days seems like a long time," she said, finishing her shaky speech, "but now I know that it's just the beginning."

As the night settled down and the Narcotics Anonymous meeting was wrapping up, Nikki felt all hugged out and was getting a little antsy to go home. Home was just a tiny one-bedroom apartment, barely larger than a studio, but it was something, all hers, and she had to get ready for a job interview the next morning. Mornings were still hard for Nikki; she no longer had the crutch of an upper to get going, and it was when she felt the worst, like the opposite of sundowners. Knowing she had to go to bed early to get through the next day, she made her way over to

Ken, who was talking to a guy named Joe. Tall, handsome, single, yet Nikki couldn't care less. These people saw her for what she was, and she wasn't sure if that was a good thing. Ken, who also happened to be tall, handsome, and single, motioned her over, wrapping her in a giant bear hug. Ken was handsome in a different way than Joe. Where Joe was tough looking and rugged, Ken seemed more like an altar boy than a recovering addict.

He whispered in her ear, "I am so proud of you, you know."

"Thanks, Ken. I'm, um, proud of me, too. And thank you—" Nikki always tried to thank him, and Ken always swatted the thanks away, leaving the words in the air like mist.

"I've told you before, God put me here to bring you peace." Ken winked at Nikki, who rolled her eyes, to lighten the weight of the words. Ken brought Joe into the conversation, telling him, "She always thinks I'm joking."

Joe laughed but looked at the chip in his hand for a moment. It was a nine-month chip, and he was just beginning to see that he could maybe, possibly sustain a life of sobriety. To Nikki, he said, "I bet he says that to all the pretty women he finds in the trash."

"Ha!" Ken lightly tapped Joe's shoulder in a fake punch. "That's why the coffee shop stays in business, then. To keep me carrying empty cups and searching for pretty women."

Nikki said her goodbyes and left the legion hall, pulling her sweatshirt around her neck to ward off the chilly air. It always made her feel uncomfortable when Ken talked like that. She only agreed to these meetings because although they were faith-based, they could still be followed without believing, and she didn't believe—how could she? She pretty much had to take care of herself when she was a child and teenager since both of her parents were hooked on drugs. She watched them, stuck in an endless cycle of being messed-up, fighting, abusing each other—both verbally and physically—making up, getting clean for a few weeks, until one or the other had a bad day and the cycle started all over again.

Nikki always figured that it would end when one of them died, and it did, only the other is still living in hell. Eight years ago, her dad overdosed on heroin and her mom, too high out to notice, much less care, left him lying in his own vomit to die. The next day, Nikki came home to a dead father and a mother who was strung out on God knows what. She called 911 and, long story short, her mother was now in prison for involuntary manslaughter, and even though it wasn't Nikki's fault, she carried tremendous guilt for that.

She was seventeen then and got put into foster care since there was no other family alive to take care of her. Well, not that she knew of, anyway. Her mom and dad weren't exactly forthcoming about their personal histories, and Nikki had never known any grandparents or aunts or uncles. With nowhere to go and no resources, she stayed with the first family who would take her, a rough-looking couple who clearly were in for the money.

Even though their oldest son thought that Nikki was there for his personal entertainment and hit on her all the time, buying her slutty outfits, and leaving condoms by her bed, "just in case," he wasn't abusing her physically. So, she stuck it out until she turned eighteen and left. Walked right out the door at 12:01 a.m. and never looked back.

A few hazy years later and here she was, unable to keep a job, with no money and almost no friends. Would God really want that for her? She doubted it, and she doubted him. As much as Ken joked about the why and how he found her lying in the dumpster, Nikki had a feeling that he meant what he said, that he was there just for her. For some reason, it both comforted and bothered her at the same time.

After she entered her apartment building and climbed the three flights of stairs to her apartment, Nikki stopped at the landing to catch her breath. One day, her goal was to be able to afford a building with an elevator. On the bulletin board on the landing, just three doors from her entrance, there was a flashy flyer, an advertisement for a psychic. Nikki rolled her eyes for the second time that night, not believing in psychic abilities any more than she believed in God. She passed by it and headed to her door, only to see the same damn flyer taped there, too. She looked around and noted that it was not on any other doors, so she yanked it off, balled it up, and flung it on the floor.

Once inside, it took about fifteen seconds for Nikki to close her door, drop her bag on the tiny kitchen counter, and hang up her keys. In that time the flyer made its way onto the floor *inside* her apartment, face up, not a crinkle on it. She stared at it and read the words *Don't go through your life with unanswered questions, grab hold of your destiny with a free reading at Wanda's Psychic Powers!* The flyer had a swirl of color through it, like a hippie kaleidoscope, and a phone number on the bottom. Nikki grabbed it and realized she had been holding her breath, as if something sinister would manifest from a simple piece of paper. She wanted to open her door to be sure the flyer she threw on the floor was still there, that it hadn't reinvented itself in her apartment, but she didn't—afraid that it wouldn't be there and then she'd have to deal with *that* bit of freaky reality.

Nikki balled up the flyer, again, and tossed it in her trash. She was nervous enough about the next day's interview and certainly didn't need any wacky psychic to tell her that. As Nikki went through her nightly routine to get ready for bed, a breeze blew through the building's hallway. She didn't know it, but there was no other flyer in the hall, and the one she threw out was again lying in perfect shape on her kitchen counter where she would find it in the morning.

4
THE BIG HOUSE

"Nicole, you know I didn't mean it like that. I just wasn't expecting this. It's a big deal."

Nikki and her mom, Janice, sat together at a little table in the visitors' room at the Big House—Nikki's fancy word for prison. She has never forgiven herself for calling 911 when her father died, thus starting the whole process of her mom being locked up. Using the term *Big House* tricked her brain, just a tiny bit, into imagining her mother elsewhere.

Nikki crossed her legs and turned from her mother, holding on to the cheap foam cup so hard it was beginning to bow. Cold coffee sloshed onto her chipped nails. "I know it's a big deal, Mom, but you didn't have to laugh. The people at NA are actually pretty cool. And Ken literally pulled me from a dumpster and took me in."

Janice shook her head and looked around her tiny world. She couldn't imagine anyone coming to rescue her, and felt a ping of jealousy toward her daughter, which made her feel a ping of guilt for the jealous feeling. Of course, she wanted better for Nicole than she had gotten, but it seemed a little too miraculous for her liking. Here her child was getting "saved" and having strange men rescue her, when all the news she had was a fresh shiner on her left eye thanks to a run-in with a wall. The wall was named Betty—the largest piece of trailer trash Janice had ever laid eyes on.

"Mom, are you even listening to me?" Nikki started bobbing her crossed leg, anxious. Even though her mom swore she was clean and not using in the Big House, she still had that look about her: quick eyes, always paranoid, too skinny. Then again, she was in *prison*, for heaven's sake.

"Yes, yes, of course I am listening to you. I'm proud of you, I am, and thankful that this Ken person found you. I'm just worried, Nicole. Men don't usually find girls in the garbage and take them home."

"He didn't take me home, Mom. He helped me to get a place to live and lined me up with some job interviews," she said, leaving out the part about her *not* getting the last one that she interviewed for. "And he lent me a little bit of cash, which I will pay back as soon as I can." Nikki tried to look her mother in the eye, the one that wasn't half-swollen shut, but her mom's gaze just wouldn't land back on her.

"And your pimp? He just let you go? That seems unlikely. There's one lady in here that had to kill her pimp for her to be free of him. That's why she's in here, actually—she got busted and thrown in prison even though she was defending herself. But she swears that she would kill him again if it meant being free of that life."

Nikki sighed. She didn't understand it, either. She had pleaded with Ken to let her either talk to Big Pete or just run away, but he insisted that he would speak with him and not to worry about it. Nikki's stomach started to hurt. Anxiety crept in as she began to question how she went from being broken in the garbage to living clean and sober in an apartment in what seemed like an instant. She thought about the words that Ken used, like *God's plan*, and she figured that he was either a do-gooding holy roller or a serial killer. Either way, she was feeling pretty healthy, and her mom was sitting in prison, so Nikki guessed whatever his motive, Ken was the better role model for her at the moment.

Janice didn't seem to notice her daughter's sudden discomfort. She continued with her story, eyes finally settling on Nikki, as she said, "Speaking of being free of that life, I really am happy for you. I just worry, is all. It's not like I can do anything to help you in here."

Again, that twist of guilt. "Mom, I'm so sorry that I called that day for Dad, I just... He was dead and I had no idea what was going on or what would happen." This was an apology that Nikki had been repeating for years.

Janice tried to reach out for Nikki, but a guard somewhere in the corner made a little *ahem* sound, reminding them that there was no touching. She settled for prolonged eye contact, something that was more intimate than hugging, in her book. "Not your fault, Nicole. I've told you that before."

It was a kind statement, Nikki knew, but she wanted more. She wanted her mom to tell her that it was her own fault, for leaving her husband to die. She wanted her to say that it was for the best because now at least she was clean and getting help. She wanted to hear her say "I love you," or at the very least, "I'm sorry for giving you such a crappy life." But those words did not happen, and by the time Nikki opened her mouth to continue the moment, Janice was looking around the room again, trying to get the guard's attention to be escorted back to her room. Her room was a cell, of course, with bars for windows, but Nikki tried not to dwell on that.

Disassociating was something that she had gotten pretty good at over the years. And then there was the undeniable fact that her mother was already trying to get away from her, so basically her mother would rather play chess or whatever the hell they did in prison with Betty than talk to her own daughter.

"Okay, well, I've got to get going," Nikki told her, letting her off the hook as usual. "Got another job interview lined up in the morning."

Janice smiled and drank the last of her coffee, handing the empty cup to Nikki. "Good luck with all that," she told her, standing up and signaling to the guard that they were finished. "I really hope you can stay clean and turn it around." At that, she turned toward the locked double doors and waited for them to be opened for her.

Nikki stood there for a moment, listening to the final *clink* of the closed doors before she could turn away. "I love you, too, Mom," she whispered to the empty space in front of her.

Once the loneliness that seized Nikki's insides subsided just a bit, she turned from the locked doors that caged her mom, threw out their cups, and went back to the check-in desk to gather her keys and purse.

Theresa, the staff member that checked Nikki in, was the same person who checked her out. She was occupied by something on her cell phone and barely glanced at Nikki as she found the cubby containing her belongings. It seemed that Theresa was almost always on duty when Nikki visited her mom, which made her feel better about the whole awkward, "my mom is in prison" reveal. Even though Theresa wasn't necessarily friendly or upbeat, with her cropped short brown hair and too-small uniform, at least she wasn't a complete stranger, and often she made an effort to share a kind word.

As Theresa dropped the keys into Nikki's outstretched hands, she took a quick break from TikTok and asked, "Did you say your last goodbye to your mother today?"

Nikki's breath made a noise as it caught in her throat. "What?" she snapped back.

Theresa looked up from her phone again and said, "Um, did you have a nice visit with your mom today? Are you all right, Nicole?"

Nikki shook her head clear. "Sorry, I must have misheard you. Yeah, it was fine. See you soon," she said and practically ran for the door as Theresa watched her almost hit the wall before the exit. Stopping short, Nikki was struck by a flyer hanging on the bulletin board. It read, in a swirl of color, "Don't go through your life with unanswered questions, grab hold of your destiny with a free reading at Wanda's Psychic Powers!"

"Wow, this psychic must be pretty desperate, advertising in prison," Nikki said to herself but out loud.

"Yes," a man's voice tickled her ear it was so close, "these folks all know their fate already."

Someone may as well have poured a bucket of ice over Nikki's head, she was that cold, with fear trickling up and down her spine as she turned around. She hadn't seen anyone else by the doors when she saw the flyer, yet there was a man, standing uncomfortably close behind her, reading over her shoulder.

The man was tall and quite large, good looking but in a scraggly way, and wore a guard's uniform. "Sorry if I startled you. I was walking in, and you almost ran me over to look at the board here," he told her. His voice was gruff, and Nikki thought that it matched his physique perfectly.

Nikki noticed that his eyes were amber, almost gold. It was unnerving.

"That's, ah, that's okay. Have a nice day." Nikki bowed out as quickly as she could, nausea rising in her gut as she left the building. She speed-walked to her bus stop, and wished she could take a hit of something to calm her nerves. The guy made her physically ill, although she couldn't explain why. She had never seen him before. He was polite, although a bit close for comfort.

It's just because he's a stranger and strangers are scary, Nikki thought, which was ironic since her last profession involved sex with those scary strangers. The drugs helped with that, though, and there was the undeniable fact that one of them did beat her up and throw her away. Right before she rounded the corner, she risked a peek over her shoulder at the prison's entrance and there he was, staring back at her, gold eyes staring into her brown ones.

Nikki fumbled, dropping her keys. She thought her heart had stopped for a second but there it was, racing like a horse in the Kentucky Derby. She bent to pick up her keys, and by the time she was upright again, he was gone.

5
LOOK INTO MY EYES

About two weeks after visiting her mom in the Big House, Nikki learned that the universe has some sneaky ways of getting what it wants. After being turned down for several jobs that she applied for, Nikki combed every newspaper she could find and called each one for an interview. She didn't care what the job was, she just needed money. It wasn't that Ken was pressuring her to pay him back—he didn't seem concerned about money at all—but she didn't feel completely comfortable relying on someone like that. It wasn't just because she had never had someone to rely on, but after her mom had asked about Big Pete and how she was able to just leave his employ, Nikki wondered more and more about what was up with Ken's kindness to her.

At the previous week's NA meeting, Nikki sat on the rigid plastic chair and listened to several other members tell their stories. She realized that she didn't know Ken's story, and asked a few of the other members, but it seemed no one could recall hearing it. Ken had been at NA longer than any of them, ran the meetings, and rarely talked about himself at all. She presumed he had shared at one point, but from what she could tell it had been a while.

She spent days thinking and doubting, circling every help wanted ad she found in the paper, calling each one, feeling more dejected by the hour as they told her that the position was either already taken or she was not qualified. When she finally got a "yes" to an interview, Nikki was elated, so excited that as she got out of a cab that same afternoon, she realized that she didn't even know the name of the place she was going, or the actual job that she applied for. All she had was an address: 5792 Moonshine Street. She liked the name of the street and thought it would be a very hip address to work at. *Heck,* she thought, *any address that is indoors is pretty awesome compared to working outside on the streets.*

As Nikki pushed the clinking doors open, she caught the shop's logo on the side window: a hippie kaleidoscope with the words *Wanda's Psychic Powers— we knew you were coming.*

"You've got to be kidding me," she said to herself, aloud. Nikki stepped into the shop and instantly felt a small vibration, like she was standing near a Tesla coil. It freaked her out and she turned to leave when she heard a little tinkling of a bell near her feet. She looked down just as a dainty little cat rubbed its body on her legs. It was all black except for a tiny triangle of white on its chest and seemed pretty friendly. Nikki bent down to pet it and noticed the collar with a tiny name tag.

"Destiny," she read. "Well, that figures." Just like when that creepy security guard spoke behind her from seemingly out of nowhere, so did the bejeweled woman that suddenly loomed behind her.

"I see you've met our little bundle of love," the woman told Nikki, who jumped at the sound of the sudden voice. Nikki had to look up to see the woman's face, as she stood six inches or more taller than herself. "Welcome to Wanda's Psychic Powers. I am Melissa. This beautiful girl here is Destiny, and you," the woman said, outstretching her arms in a regal stance. "You must be Nicole," she said, bowing slightly.

"Ah, yes. Nikki, actually. How did you know?"

Melissa pointed to the huge sign on the wall that said, in all caps and glowed neon green: PSYCHIC.

"Um..." Nikki stopped herself from rolling her eyes, but Melissa smiled anyway, knowing a skeptic when she saw one.

"It's true, I am a psychic," Melissa told her. "But we also had an appointment. You called about the job, remember?"

Nikki laughed, feeling like an idiot but also relieved. "I think I have an appointment with Wanda?" she asked.

"That's impossible. Wanda is no longer with us. This is my place now, but she wasn't happy with me when I changed the name to 'Melissa's Psychic Powers,' so I changed it back."

For some reason, Nikki was intrigued, and just had to ask, "So, you bought the business from her, and she won't let you change the name? Is that even legal?"

Again, that smile from Melissa, as if she was toying with Nikki but in a friendly way. "Well, I do own the business, but I didn't buy it from her. She left it to me, which was very kind, so I tend to obey her wishes."

Nikki was confused, but understanding began to creep up her spine in a trickle of cold. "She's dead?" she asked. Ever so slightly, she lifted each foot and placed it back down, slightly pointed at the door. She was ready to jet. Destiny curled up in the corner and began to lick her paws, looking bored.

"Well, she doesn't like to think of herself as dead. She's just not in her body anymore. For some reason, Wanda insists that she has work to do yet while here," Melissa explained this as though she were speaking to a child. And in ways, she was, knowing that even adults, or especially adults, had a tough time understanding what cannot be seen or easily explained.

Nikki crossed her arms, as if insulted, as she repeated the statement that she knew to be true: "But dead is dead." She couldn't help but think of her father, his body cold when she found him, glazed-over eyes staring at nothing. If he were able to be a spirit, he would have stayed, wouldn't he? Would he just leave her in this shit show of a life if he had a *choice*? Thoughts spun out of control as she tried to control her breathing. For the first time in weeks, Nikki wanted a hit of something to calm her nerves.

Melissa shook her head, knowingly, as if she saw Nikki's every thought and already had the answers. She reached out and touched her shoulder, her hand warm, the gesture making Nikki's knees soften and tears well in her eyes. "Dead is *not* dead, actually. Sometimes we move on to heal, reflect, and wait for our time to return to Earth, and sometimes, we choose to stick around a little while, usually because our jobs aren't done," she tried to explain yet stuck to the basics, not wanting to give too much information on an already confusing matter. Not so soon.

What Melissa told her made enough sense, if you believed in reincarnation and all that, but Nikki still didn't understand why her dad would go *heal and reincarnate* before making sure that she was okay. She wasn't okay—she used to get high and try to *will* him to her, and now she did not want to hear that he had a choice and he left her all alone.

"You know," she told Melissa, taking a step back, "I don't think that this job is right for me. I don't know anything about what you're talking about. I don't know what I could possibly do to help you."

Suddenly all business, Melissa recited the job description, "Basic office help includes answering phones, making appointments, inventory, ringing up customers, and light cleaning. Customer care and confidentiality a must, everything else can be taught on the job."

Sounded easy enough, Nikki knew, and she really needed a job. Plus, the cat was really cute. It had been a long time since Nikki was around an animal that actually liked her. The last cat she was around was an alley cat who would claw at Nikki if she came too close, and who stole her food at night.

"Look into my eyes, Nikki. All you need is an open mind and you and I will get along fine. You were meant to walk through these doors," Melissa told her, adding in what Nikki couldn't refuse, "I also have a sign-on bonus. It's $500 when you start, and $500 after ninety days."

Nikki laughed. "Do you win everyone over with the 'Look into my eyes' bit?" she asked, already calculating what she would do with her first check.

"Nope, first time I've ever used it," Melissa told her, sticking out her hand for Nikki to shake. "Welcome to Wanda's. I can't wait to get to know you."

When Nikki was leaving the shop, she had a tentative first week schedule, a book on chakras, and a medicine pouch filled with herbs, a citrine crystal, and a penny. She had no idea what any of that meant, but she promised to keep it in her pocket for the rest of the week. She paused at the door and looked back at the interior of the shop. Melissa had already disappeared into the back, so she had a moment to just rest her eyes on the eclectic objects. Crystals, candles, incense, oils, tarot cards—if someone were visiting this shop, they would not leave empty-handed. The best part for Nikki was the smell, a background of sweet incense and an oil that she could not place, so she promised herself she would find out what it was when she started work, and bring home that very scent.

Destiny got up from her place in the corner, stretched, and walked toward the door. Nikki gave behind her ears a scratch and said, "Thanks for your hospitality." The cat just blinked at her and walked away, as if escorting people to the door was a natural thing to do.

As Nikki softly shut the door, she thought she heard a whisper pass in front of her. "Welcome, Nicole," a soft, female voice said. Nikki turned around to see if Melissa was at the door, or perhaps a window, but she didn't see her anywhere.

Wanda wanted to say more, but didn't want to frighten her away, knowing in the coming weeks they would have a great deal to talk about.

The moment passed, Nikki distracted by the good news of finally getting a job, and she walked toward the bus stop, unaware that Melissa had stepped out of the shop to watch her go and had a heated discussion with the empty space in front of her.

6
THE PATH LESS TRAVELED

In the week leading up to her first day at Wanda's Psychic Powers, Nikki was a bundle of nerves. This job meant so much to her, not only because she got it on her own, but because it was legal and moral. And safe. Plus, she would be making enough money to start to pay Ken back. In another year, she figured she would be completely debt free, owing nothing to anyone, financially anyway. It was a great feeling, and despite her inclination to be on the lookout for something to go wrong, Nikki felt hopeful. She even bought a little bag of organic cat treats for Destiny.

That hopeful feeling was dampened when, on the morning before Nikki was supposed to start, she woke up in the midst of a nightmare. In it, she was running through the woods and her clothes had blood all over them, although she knew it was not hers. A faceless man was hunting her, calling after her, only he had her name wrong. He was calling the name Julietta, but in a singsong voice, "Juliet- ta, Juliet-ta, where are you? Come out, come out, wherever you are."

She had tears running down her face. She felt as if she knew the man and wanted to go to him, but he was clearly trying to hurt her. Confused and exhausted from running, she hunkered down beneath a pricker bush, eyes squeezed shut, trying to calm her breathing and quelch her impulse to scream.

His voice again, menacing yet soothing, as if he was playing with a small child. He called out, "You can't hide from me forever, Julietta." *Crunch, crunch, crunch,* the sound of his boots was coming closer, and as Nikki tried to get farther under the bush, blood-soaked clothes snagging the prickers that caused little gashes of their own, she knew that he had found her.

With a burst of adrenaline, Nikki pushed herself up, ripped herself away from the prickers, and ran full speed into the darkening woods. Only about a yard behind her, the man yelled for her again, only this time, he stopped her dead in her tracks.

This time it was her own name that she heard, as he hollered, "Nicole!" and when she stopped and turned around to face him, the only part of his face that she could make out was his mouth. He smiled, and said, "Gotcha," moving toward her quickly now.

Nicole was too terrified to move, and just as the man reached her and she started to make out his features, her alarm rang in her ears. She woke up, panting and scared.

"What in the holy hell was that all about?" she asked herself as she turned the alarm off and rolled out of bed. Ever since Ken rescued her from the dumpster, Nicole always got right out of bed in the morning. She was almost afraid of what would happen if she hit snooze and turned over in the comfort of her bed, as if she needed the momentum of being a good person and didn't want to let her guard down.

Once she was up and showered, Nikki tried to decide what to do with her last day of freedom before she was tied down to a job. As excited as she was to start, and as intrigued as she was by Melissa and her predecessor, Nikki had a small longing for the simpler life of getting high and hooking up for a living. Immediately regretting the thought, she decided to reach out to Ken. He was always a good antidote to her wild, reckless side.

Although it was a Sunday and she figured he would be busy, Ken answered Nikki's text right away and suggested they have lunch at a little bistro about two blocks from her apartment. It was just like him, to be there when she needed him, at any time. She had wondered in the beginning of their friendship—saviorship?—if he was attracted to her sexually or romantically, but she didn't think so. He had more of a big brother vibe to him, and for some reason she always felt like she had to make him proud. She thought back to the feeling of unease that she felt about him while with her mom at the Big House and felt silly. Nikki acknowledged to herself that the prison environment breeds mistrust, not to mention her mom's line of questioning, and that she shouldn't take any of her fears or doubts too seriously when she's there.

As soon as she saw him, sitting at a little table just inside the bistro, Nikki knew that something was wrong. Ken looked like he hadn't slept in days, and he looked nervous, jittery. Praying that he wasn't using, Nikki took the seat across from him, noticing that he didn't even see her until she was sitting down. She had never seen him like this.

As soon as they made eye contact, he visibly softened. "Oh Nicole, thank God," he said, taking her hands in his.

Nikki found it weird that he called her Nicole but figured it was just this odd state he was in. "Are you all right?" she asked him. "You look sick, or scared, or..." She let the sentence hang in the air, not daring to accuse him of being on something.

Ken took his hands back from Nikki and covered his face for a moment, seemingly wiping his features away. In a flash, he looked fine, and Nikki was reminded of a cartoon character and how he seemed to reshape his face.

"Seriously, Ken, what's going on?" she asked him.

"I just haven't been sleeping very well lately. And last night, well, I had a nightmare about you. The details are fuzzy, but I was so worried about you."

Nikki felt a tiny pinprick of something unpleasant at the nape of her neck. "I had a nightmare last night, too. Someone was hunting me, and he called me by someone else's name. And I was covered in blood, but it wasn't my own. What was yours about? And why didn't you just call me if you were worried?"

She noticed that Ken flushed a bit. "I-I don't really remember my dream, but you were definitely in it. You were in danger, and I was trying to find you," he told her. "And I didn't call you because I didn't want to worry you. Which is silly, I know. I guess I've just been off lately," he confessed.

Nikki was at a loss for what to say and was grateful when the waitress came. It wasn't until the waitress flipped her pad open that Nikki realized she was starving, and she wanted whatever scent was floating around the small room. She said as much to the waitress, and they ended up ordering two cups of coffee and two slices of spinach and bacon quiche. While they were ordering, Nikki stole glances at Ken, wondering what was going on with him. While they waited for the food, she decided to distract both of them with first-day jitters small talk. She thought that Ken would be against the idea of working for a psychic, seeing how religious he seemed to be, but he seemed genuinely interested in all things metaphysical.

Ken asked her a ton of questions and wanted to know everything; how long Melissa was a practicing psychic (Nikki had no idea), if she was the real deal and could actually *see* things (Nikki didn't know that either, but Melissa did seem to know that money was a good enough motivator to get her to take the job), and which fortune-telling methods she used (*seriously?* Nikki thought.)

Now Ken was schooling Nikki in the art of fortune-telling. "There are the usual tarot cards and rune stones, of course, but also pendulum readings, dream interpretation, astrology, and even tassology," he told her.

"I'm sorry, what?" Nikki interrupted, wondering again if Ken was on something.

"Tassology, tasseography—it's the art of tea leaf reading," Ken explained.

Nikki couldn't help but roll her eyes at him. "Tea leaf reading, Ken? Really?"

Ken didn't even seem to notice her sarcasm. "Well, not only tea, technically. You can also find answers in coffee grounds and wine sediments."

"Okay, look, I have no idea what kind of fortune-telling Melissa does. I haven't even started work yet. And now I'm feeling overwhelmed, and all she said I had to do was answer the phone and book appointments." Nikki was feeling annoyed and confused, wondering how on Earth a holy roller like Ken would know about this stuff, and why.

She decided to ask him as much, and his answer only left her with more questions. He paused for a moment and said, "Things are not always black and white in life, Nikki. I am religious, yes. But I pull my beliefs from a very old knowledge and am not tied down by what society wants us to believe in this moment. I see things differently, and have a very specific purpose in my life. Sometimes, to get what you want, you need to learn to take the path less traveled."

"Okay, now I'm just more confused about you, and honestly, I don't see how fortune-telling has anything to do with religion."

Ken laughed and sat up straighter in preparation for the waitress who was walking over with their food. "I might have knowledge, but I don't have all the answers. What I look for is signs to tell me if I'm doing the right thing, if I'm helping the right people, if I'm saving or condemning." He stopped talking when the waitress put the plates of quiche down in front of them. "Thanks so much," he said. Ken picked up his fork and seemed to be extremely interested in his food for a moment. Nikki wondered if he was reading the spinach leaves, not really knowing if Ken was a kook or a sage, or something in between.

Trying to lighten the mood a little bit, Nikki jokingly asked Ken what he saw in his slice of quiche. He didn't laugh but slowly turned his plate around, to show her what he was staring at. A stray piece of spinach lay across his slice, with a little *T* on top, so that it resembled an arrow. Not just resembled, the tiny green leaf actually looked like a hastily drawn arrow.

"When she put this down," Ken said, spinning his plate around again, "it was pointing directly at you. You see, signs everywhere."

Nikki was tired of feeling apprehensive. "But what does it mean?" she asked him.

Ken picked up his fork and took a bite. "Don't know, but all signs point to you at the moment," he said, and winked at her.

Nikki was about to quip back when her cell rang. She usually silenced her phone when she went into a restaurant. She grabbed it from her pocket and swiped left, not recognizing the number. Before she was able to shove it back in her pocket and take a bite of her food, the voice mail sound went off, which was weird because not that many people bothered leaving a message. She listened to it quickly, ducking her head so she didn't feel rude.

Nikki listened to the message and put her phone back in her pocket. She looked normal to Ken, only she was ghost white and expressionless. "Are you okay?" he asked her.

She shook her head no. "That was Theresa from the Big House—sorry, from the prison where my mom is at. She said that I need to come right away, that something has happened to my mom."

While sitting at the bistro with Ken, before she even had a chance to try her lunch, Nikki's life was forever changed.

7
ORPHANED

Nikki couldn't feel her legs as she went through security at the Big House. She felt off, as if she had vertigo, but it encompassed her entire being. The message she got from Theresa was cryptic, but she knew that something was terribly wrong. It was hushed, clear that Theresa was not supposed to be making the call. All she said was, "Nicole, you gotta get here now—something terrible has happened to your mom."

Theresa wasn't at the front desk as she usually was. No one that Nikki recognized was at that station—instead there were a bunch of men dressed in plain black suits. Not cops, she didn't think, and no FBI jackets, nothing to identify who they were. One of them intercepted her with a quick, "I'm sorry miss, but there's no visiting hours today."

Nikki didn't budge. "I want to see my mother," she said to the man, who was now standing uncomfortably close to her. He was at least a foot taller than she was at five-foot-four, and thin with a long neck, so that he looked like an ostrich intimidating his prey.

"But I got a call—" Nikki started to explain when she saw two of the men behind the desk glance at one another.

"A call from who?" the tall man asked, interrupting her before she could finish her sentence, to which she would have already said who the call was from. The rudeness of the man made her pause.

"Um, I'm not sure who it was. But they said that something happened to my mom." The men just stared at her, so she continued. "Her name is Janice Ingles."

Nikki heard the man breathe out, through his nose, in a huff. "Come with me, miss," he said, gesturing to a set of doors that Nikki had never been through. When visiting her mom, the process was always the same; security check, drop your items off at the desk and sign in, make a left, and wait to be buzzed in through the thick metal doors that led to the visitors' room. Nikki never even noticed the doors to the right, and when the buzz sounded and they swung open, she flinched.

The tall man walked in front of her but to the side, so that he could see her in his peripheral vision. This part of the prison was so clean that all Nikki could smell was disinfectant, and the floors sparkled. It was obvious that it was not a place for the inmates, since her mom always complained that the prison smelled musty. The short hallway housed a few small offices and ended with a giant conference room. They entered, and Nikki recognized Peter Hesson, the warden, right away. She had never met the man, but she saw his picture on the prison's website. She had spent a lot of time on that site when her mom was first convicted.

The warden was ending a phone call as they walked in, presumably with the men at the front desk telling him that she was on her way. He smiled and rose to greet them, and though he was almost a foot shorter than her escort, his stance was imposing. Militant and stern.

He came around the conference table and took her hand, speaking firmly yet softly. "Nicole, I am Warden Hesson. I am so sorry to meet like this," he told her.

Nikki was immediately on guard, wondering why this man would know her name.

"Like what, exactly?" Nikki's mind reeled, not knowing what was happening but knowing that if it weren't terrible and had to do with her mom, she wouldn't even be there.

The warden shifted uncomfortably, and said, "Maybe you should sit down, and we can talk."

"Or you can tell me where my mom is, and why I'm even in here." Nikki was feeling panicked.

The warden sighed. Nikki would never forget that sigh, it was a clear admission that something terrible happened. "I'm so sorry, Nicole. Janice was in a terrible accident this afternoon. I'm afraid, well, I'm afraid that she has passed."

Just like that, the cards were on the table. Just like that, Nikki's entire life was forever changed. She was parentless, an orphan. "My, um, my mom's dead?" Nikki said the words out loud, yet they sounded strange to her ears. Stunned, Nikki found herself sitting after all, in a hard-backed chair that was the opposite of comforting. "What kind of accident?" she asked the warden, although it didn't really matter. Her mom was dead and the act of asking questions seemed to help numb whatever emotional storm was coming.

The warden sat next to Nikki and shifted, uncomfortable. "That is still under investigation," he told her stiffly.

"Well, what in the hell does that mean?" Nikki asked, fresh tears making their way down her cheeks. "Did she...did she hurt herself?" That was one worry that Nikki always had; that her mom would kill herself in prison.

The warden frowned. "No, no, nothing like that. What I am about to tell you is classified information, and as long as the investigation is going on, we will need you to stay silent. Is that understood?"

Nikki nodded, silently.

"I'm sorry, Nicole, but I will need for you to answer before I can proceed." The warden was all business.

Nikki said yes, expecting the worst. Maybe another prisoner killed her mom, and she was found in the shower, naked. Or perhaps she died all alone at the lunch table, and no one even noticed her until the room was clearing out. All sorts of scenarios ran through Nikki's brain, and not one of them was as bad as the truth.

Warden Hesson was a man who tended to lay the facts out and let the chips fall where they may. That was exactly how he told Nikki how her mother had been murdered. "Your mother was found with a broken neck, in the laundry facility, at 1300 this afternoon."

"Thirteen hundred?" Nikki asked, feeling like she was floating above the room, hearing the conversation from different ears.

"Sorry, miss. That's one o'clock this afternoon." The warden broke eye contact, and Nikki knew he was leaving something out.

"So, who killed her?" she asked, needing to know, yet knowing that it didn't matter. Knowing who, or why, or how wouldn't bring her mom back.

Shifting in the seat so that it creaked, the warden answered softly and simply, telling her, "I don't know."

Nikki didn't believe that. "You don't know? Well, don't you have cameras in there?"

"We do, yes. They happened to be down during time of death." The warden looked uncomfortable.

Something changed at that moment for Nikki, and she had no idea why. She felt a tiny prick of fear in her stomach, and it traveled up her spine and into her skull. The weight of what the warden was saying began to settle on her shoulders. Nikki knew that the prison was extremely diligent about their security, and for the cameras to be down right when her mom was killed could not have been a coincidence. "So, what you're telling me, warden," Nikki said, sitting up taller in her chair, "is that my mom could have been killed by staff of this prison? Who was with her? Have they gotten fingerprints?"

Closing his eyes briefly, as if he were centering himself for the words he was about to speak, the warden managed to hold eye contact with Nikki as he told her, "Your mother was found in one of our industrial-sized washing machines. It was put on a special sanitizing cycle that we use for prisoners' bedding and towels. The temperature runs around one hundred and fifty degrees. Your mother has third degree burns all over her body and is missing some skin. I don't know that there is much evidence to be recovered."

"Oh my God," was all that Nikki could muster. She stared at the warden dumbly, the images in her head overtaking her ability to speak. In her mind, she imagined her mom's body, clunking around and around in near boiling water. Her mom, floating, dead, eyes wide open. Skinned. She saw her father, lying in the froth of his own insides, waiting for her to find him. It was too much for her, as old memories meshed with new images.

Nikki looked at the warden, who was looking less stern and more concerned, as the peripheral of her vision started to fade. "Nicole, I'm so sorry," he was saying to her. "Nicole, are you all right? Special Agent Higgins, I need a little assistance in here."

Nikki heard him speak to her, heard the call for help, but shock took over her body and before the warden or the agent came to her rescue, she slipped out of consciousness and slid out of the chair and onto the floor.

The last thing Nikki remembered before the cold, black nothingness overcame her was the faintest scent of freshly washed laundry. It reminded her of her mom, when Nikki was a little girl, hanging their clothes to dry outside on a sunny day. The memory faded away and as she lost awareness, she took with her the image of her mom, covered in suds, crying for help.

8
GOTCHA

Murder is unsettling, and Nikki didn't know what to do with herself. It had been two days since her mom had been killed, and she still had no answers. It didn't look like she was going to get many either, since they couldn't pull any camera footage or fingerprints from the scene. Her mom had been killed, she had no idea why or by whom, and it was driving her crazy. To make things worse, she had to miss her first few days of work. She couldn't pull herself together.

Nikki went from sobbing in her bed to pacing her apartment. Ken called and texted, and even showed up to knock at her door, but she didn't answer. Her new boss, Melissa, called a few times as well, but even though she knew she should answer, she couldn't make herself do it. She felt alone, and her loneliness became an unquenchable thirst in a wasteland of sand.

The day was growing dark, and Nikki couldn't believe that two days had passed so quickly. Even doing nothing but sleeping, pacing, and making the most basic of funeral arrangements—luckily the prison was paying for the expense, which Nikki found suspicious—two days of being motherless flew by. That wasn't fair, she knew, she wasn't motherless, exactly. She still had a mom, technically. But her mom was dead, so she sure felt like she didn't have one.

There is something about losing the matriarch of a family that can cause people to question their future. Even though Janice was not a great ruler of their little family, she was still at the top. With no moral compass, Nikki no longer knew what kind of person she wanted to be. Until then, she hadn't even realized that the part of her (a small part, sure, but it was still there) that wanted to be clean and sober and off the streets was to make her mom proud. She wanted to do better than her mom did, and when the prison sentence ended Nikki had visions of them starting over somewhere. Without that compass, the needle didn't know where to point. Which meant Nikki was getting thirsty, and not for water. She wanted alcohol or some coke. Even a joint would do. She picked up her phone and watched the ticking clock on the wall. Tick, tick, tick. One text to her old friends and she would be feeling no pain. Tick, tick, the liquor store was right around the corner from her apartment. Tick. Nikki felt defeated, and much to Ken's relief, she texted him back.

I'LL BE AT THE MEETING TOMORROW. I REALLY NEED IT.

Ken texted her back so quickly that she imagined him holding his phone for hours, waiting to hear from her. It made Nikki smile.

I LOOK FORWARD TO SEEING YOU. I'M HERE WHENEVER YOU NEED ME, ANYTIME.

With that decision made, Nikki felt proud of herself, and wondered if her mom was around to be proud of her, too. She thought about what Melissa had told her, about what happens when we die, and the choices people make. She was about to go down the rabbit hole of unanswered questions when a knock at her door made her jump.

When Nikki put her hand on the bolt of her door to unlock it, she paused. She had been so shocked over the death of her mom that she hadn't thought to be afraid. But standing there, with an unknown visitor on the other side, little tendrils of fear made their way into Nikki's thoughts. "Who is it?" she called through the door, timidly.

"Hi, Nicole. It's Theresa, from the prison." She sounded a little out of breath, and even though it was strange that Theresa was knocking on her door, Nikki was not afraid of her and let her in.

"Um, hi," was all Nikki could say. She hadn't seen anyone since she got the news and knew that she probably looked awful. "I didn't get a chance to find you the other day, to thank you for calling me."

Theresa nodded, glanced around the little apartment, and looked just as awkward as Nikki felt. Theresa was taller than her by a few inches, so Nikki had to look up at her when she spoke. Since Nikki usually saw Theresa sitting behind a desk, it was odd to view her from a different angle. At the prison, Theresa was usually bold and confident, and it was jarring for Nikki to see her in these surroundings, looking quiet and uncomfortable. When she finally spoke, she did not use the assertive voice that was normally heard, but a soft, timid tone, almost afraid.

"I wanted to tell you in person. I am so sorry about what happened to your mom," Theresa said.

Nikki thought she looked like she was going to cry. She didn't think that her mom really even knew Theresa—it's not like the prisoners have much contact with the staff that works on the other side of the giant metal doors.

Nikki tried to smile, but it looked more like a grimace. "Thank you," she said, and took a chance by asking the question that no one would answer. "Do you know what happened? I can't get a straight answer. All I know is that my mom's body was so damaged that there isn't much evidence." Nikki shivered at the visual of her mom. She pictured her all the time, going round and round in a huge washing machine, suds penetrating her body. Beating her up. She shook her head to try to get rid of the image. Nikki didn't know how she would ever do laundry again.

Theresa surprised her by asking, "Can we sit down? I have something to show you."

Suddenly nervous, Nikki led Theresa to the small sitting area and gestured to one side of the hand-me-down couch that Ken had brought over when she first moved in. She sat on the other side but faced Theresa and folded her legs under her as she tried to take deep breaths to calm her racing heart.

"Part of my job at the prison is to read incoming and outgoing mail, to and from the prisoners. They write it and I read it to make sure that there are no escape plans hidden in the words, drug deals, or directives to commit a crime, basically. Then I send them off." Theresa pulled a well-read-looking letter from her pocket and handed it to Nikki. "This letter is for you," she said, handing the paper over.

Nikki took it but continued to stare at Theresa. "Why didn't I get this then, if it's to me?" she asked.

"Because I think this is why she was killed. I put this letter in a folder to show my supervisor, and before I could go through those channels, your mom was dead."

The words floated around the room like dust. Nikki wanted to swat them away.

"And why are you giving this to me? Did you show the cops, or whoever those men were at the prison?" Nikki held the letter in her hands but didn't open it. She knew that she had to, but her mom's final words to her were something that she was not expecting, and not prepared for. She wanted Theresa to leave, so that she could open the letter in private.

Theresa shifted on the couch and spit out the next sentence as if she had to force herself to say the words. "I hid the letter. I feel like I'd be in danger it if were discovered."

"So why are you bringing it to me?" Nikki asked, a sense of dread funneling down her body.

"Because you're in danger, Nicole. I think someone is after you."

"Me?" Nikki didn't understand, and she was almost afraid to unfold the letter in her shaking hands. She looked at the paper, standard white college ruled, nothing special. She looked up and made eye contact with Theresa, who surprised Nikki by asking if her door was locked.

It wasn't, and Nikki got up and locked the doorknob, pulling the dead bolt across with a click. Quietly, she sat back down and opened the letter. She was confused at first by the usual greeting and talking about nothing—what she ate for breakfast, how she was excited for their next visit, things that she never, ever wrote about in her letters. Right in the middle of the letter, her mom's tone changed completely, and the real message was there, almost as if her mom hoped that whoever was reading the mail that day would get bored and stop halfway through. She read:

Nikki, I'm so scared. I had a run-in with one of the guards yesterday. He walked past me while I was putting a book away in the library and he did a double take, like he knew me from somewhere. He sniffed me—like, actually sniffed me like a dog—and said that he's been looking for me for a long time. I have never seen this guy in my life, I swear. I tried to flirt with him, hoping that he was looking to get lucky and in turn give me some perks, but he grabbed my wrist and told me that he'd see me again soon.

I thought it was over when he started to walk away, but he circled back and asked me if my birthday was June 6. It was the oddest question and I told him no, but that was my daughter's birthday. All he said was, "Ah, gotcha." Then he smiled at me, and I looked into his eyes, and I swear to Christ they were black. Like completely black. And he said, "I'll give her your regards."

I don't know what that means, but I think he's looking for you now. Please don't come here to see me for a while. He doesn't know what you look like or anything about you except for your birthday.

If someone is reading this, please send to my daughter. I love you, Nicole. Please stay safe.

Love, Mom

Nikki had to read the letter twice to comprehend the message, and the thoughts started spinning through her mind. Some jerk scared her mom badly enough for her to write her a letter, in hope that it would somehow make it to her. Doing so probably got her killed. Someone was maybe, possibly, looking for her, but she had no idea why. Or who. Her mom could have been overreacting but then again, she was dead so most likely not.

And there were those words that she had been yearning for, for so long. *I love you, Nicole.*

"Nicole? Are you all right?" Theresa had moved closer to her, concerned.

Nikki didn't realize that she had been crying, and wiped at her eyes while shaking her head no.

"What are we supposed to do with this?" she asked Theresa. "Should we give it to someone? Get some help?"

Theresa answered quickly, as if she'd known this question would come. "Hell no. There is no useful information in there, really. Your mom does a great job of warning you that you are in danger but a shitty job of describing the guy who scared her. And since we have no idea who that may be, I wouldn't feel safe handing this over to anyone."

This made sense to Nikki, especially since she had an inherent mistrust of authority figures. "So, what do I do now?" she asked, folding the letter nervously.

"Not what do *you* do, Nikki. What do *we* do. I'm involved now, and I'm not going to just ditch you with this. I'll do some investigating of my own at the prison. We'll figure this out."

Nikki smiled at Theresa, an almost-stranger who was now helping her. It seemed like that happened for Nikki a lot. "Thank you. Really," she said, tears flowing freely now. With Nikki, once the dam was broken, there was nothing she could do to stop herself from crying until she was all dried up.

Failing at small talk, Theresa left the apartment with a stern warning to Nikki about locking the doors and watching her back. "Don't you worry about that," Nikki assured her, anxious about being alone. They hugged awkwardly, and then Nikki shut and locked the door.

After rereading her mom's letter for about the twentieth time, Nikki fell asleep on the couch, the paper falling to the floor. She was back in the same nightmare that she had just before her mom was killed. That voice, calling to her, searching for her in the woods.

"You can't hide from me forever, Julietta." The dream replayed, but this time, just as Nikki was fighting to wake up, the man caught her. Black eyes bore into her soul as he whispered in her ear, "Gotcha."

9
HO'OPONOPONO

The funeral for Janice Ingles had four attendants: Nikki, Theresa, Ken, and Melissa. Five people, if one counted the pastor, which Nikki did not. She wasn't expecting a terrific turnout but thought that the lack of attendance was a truly devastating look into how people viewed her mom. Janice had had friends and a job before falling down the slippery slope of addiction, yet it was clear what society thought of her now, even in death.

When the pastor ended his brief burial speech with, "And may she forever rest in peace," Nikki saw Melissa close her eyes and shake her head, just a bit, as if she knew something that no one else did.

The day was damp and overcast, and the cemetery was otherwise empty. After the pastor finished with his tasks, he shook Nikki's hand and looked, no, peered into her eyes as he told her, "I'm so sorry for your loss." He walked away, Bible in hand, and moments later, the little group of mourners was joined by two grave attendants who began the work of lowering the casket into the ground.

As the casket—little more than a bare box—was lowered, the wind kicked up and for the second time since hearing the news of her mom's murder, Nikki smelled the unmistakable scent of laundry detergent. She leaned into Ken, who was standing the closest to her, and whispered, "Do you smell that?"

Ken sniffed. "Smell what?"

"The air smells like laundry detergent, doesn't it?" she asked, and the scent was so strong to her that it filled her nose.

Shaking his head no, Ken softly took Nikki's hand in his. He told her, "I don't smell anything but damp dirt."

As Nikki breathed in again, the wind carried the scent away. She felt a breeze stir around her feet and travel up her body, and once the air around her settled, the smell was gone. She saw Melissa glance at her, and wondered if she smelled it, too.

Once the casket was in the ground and covered with dirt and a little tuft of fake grass, the grave attendants gathered their straps and tools and left, only nodding to Nikki as they walked off. She turned to her friends, each of them strangers to one another but joined together to support her, and felt completely bewildered. Nikki didn't know what to do next, with the business of burying her mom complete, and she felt lost.

Theresa was the first one to break the silence of the moment, by telling Nikki that she had better get back to work. "I told them that I had to run out for a doctor's appointment," Theresa told her, and while they hugged goodbye, she whispered in Nikki's ear, "I'm keeping my eyes open."

As they watched her walk away, Nikki realized that Ken and Melissa had not even been introduced. "I'm so sorry," she told them. "Ken, this is Melissa, my new boss, and Melissa, this is Ken, my..." she trailed off, not knowing quite what to call him, certainly not wanting her new boss to know their history together. "My friend," she finished.

"It's okay, Nicole." Melissa reached out and touched her arm. "You've got a few things on your plate."

As soon as Nikki felt Melissa's hand on her arm, she felt a weird tingling sensation there, as if she could feel the energy of the touch before the actual touch. It felt...mystical, which felt appropriate since Nikki was entering the world of all things magical.

Ken and Melissa made quick eye contact and Ken told Nikki, "We actually have met. Well, not officially, but we have seen each other in Wanda's Psychic Powers before."

"*You've* been to Wanda's?" Nikki asked, surprised.

Ken laughed shyly and told her, "Yes well, you may have noticed I have a slight fascination with metaphysics."

Nikki thought back to Ken's inquisition just days earlier at the bistro and said, "Well, your line of questioning makes more sense now."

Ken held his hand out to Melissa and said, "It's nice to see you again. I was sorry to hear of Wanda's passing."

Melissa took his hand and told him, "Thank you, I miss her every day. And it's nice to see you, as well. You haven't been in the shop since, well, since it's been just me."

"Life sure does move quickly, doesn't it?" Ken said. Nikki thought his answer was vague, but then again, a lot of what Ken said was that way.

Suddenly she craved the scents of the little psychic shop and wanted to go to work. She said as much, and Melissa looked delighted.

"It beats standing in a cemetery all day," Melissa said, hooking arms with Nikki. It was a comfortable gesture, and although they were just beginning to get to know each other, Nikki quite liked it.

They started to walk away but stopped when they realized that Ken was not following. He was standing over the new grave, whispering what sounded like a prayer. Nikki and Melissa glanced at each other, and walked to Ken, still arm in arm.

Ken's head was bowed, his eyes were closed, and he chanted, "I love you. I'm sorry. Please forgive me. Thank you." He said this over and over, at least six times before Nikki finally nudged him and asked, "What on Earth are you saying, Ken?"

Ken opened his eyes. He was not crying, but his eyes were watery, and he said, "This is Ho'oponopono, the prayer of forgiveness."

"Ho'o what?" Nikki asked, looking at Melissa who just shrugged.

"Ho'oponopono. It is an ancient Hawaiian prayer of forgiveness and healing."

Nikki looked at Ken as if he had lost his mind. "But you didn't even know my mom. You don't need her forgiveness," she told him, adding, "I might, but you do not."

Ken smiled. "This tradition tells us that all of life is connected. I am not asking forgiveness from your mom, but for and with her, speaking to the divine, for the past, the present and the future. Today, I am sorry for your loss, for what happened to your mom, and for the actions of others. I ask forgiveness not for myself but for everyone involved, so that healing may occur."

Nikki nodded as if she understood, although she did not. Still, it sounded nice, and the gesture was sweet. She leaned into Ken and kissed him on the cheek. "Thank you," she told him, and to the gravesite, she said, "Mom, I love you. I'm sorry. Please forgive me. Thank you."

Together with Melissa, Nikki linked arms with Ken and turned away from the grave. It was time to move on, and for the first time in her life, Nikki felt strong.

As they walked away, past the rows of headstones, Nikki looked back at her mom's gravesite. She was distracted by a quick movement just out of her line of sight. She thought that she saw a man standing alone on the far side of the cemetery, but he stepped behind a cluster of trees as she turned. She stopped walking, and both Ken and Melissa turned to see what she was looking at. All their gazes landed on the cluster of trees in the distance. Nikki took a step in that direction, but Melissa held on to her arm, not letting her go.

"It feels sinister back there, doesn't it?" Melissa asked, her gaze still on the unseen. "It's important to remember that while we cannot see all things, we can absolutely feel them. Intuition will lead you to find the answers you seek, Nicole, but it is also there to protect you from danger."

Hearing her, Nikki stood her ground, not moving forward, yet not turning her back to the spot. She was certain she saw someone, and Melissa was right, it didn't feel safe.

"Let's get to work," she told Melissa, who looked relieved. "Maybe there's other ways to find my answers."

· · · · ·

As Nikki, Melissa, and Ken walked away from the cemetery and out of sight, Hadeon stepped away from the safety of the trees and strode to Janice's gravesite.

Kneeling, he plunged his hands into the fresh dirt and rubbed his fingers through the soil. When he saw Nikki stop and look at him, his brain shut off and instinct took over. *Kill her. Kill her. Kill her.* The words played over and over yet he didn't know why.

In his youth, Hadeon was known as a kind soul with violent tendencies, uncontrollable at times yet soft-spoken and endearing. His father had abandoned them when Hadeon was born, and his mother died when he was just five, leaving him, an only child, to endure multiple group homes and eventually mental institutions, until he turned eighteen and lived in the shadows of society, getting odd jobs to support himself.

Just a few months previous, Hadeon picked a newspaper up from the street and saw a help-wanted advertisement as a custodian in a prison that was just blocks from his small studio apartment. Something pulled him to apply, so he did. Lucky for him, whoever was processing applicants didn't do much digging and they not only offered him the job but gave him full access to the prison.

Hadeon didn't know anything about destiny or purpose, he just followed his instinct and acted on his impulses. And at that moment, as he washed his hands in the dirt of the woman he had murdered, Hadeon yearned for the woman he saw moments ago.

10
MUDDY AURA

Amethyst, citrine, smoky quartz. Crystals to focus, crystals to balance, crystals to protect. Mountain sage, clary sage, white sage. Alter items. Nikki's head was spinning, and it was only her second week working at Wanda's Psychic Powers. She had categorized and inventoried every item in the shop, learning what everything was and how it helped to heal. Doing this made her feel refreshed, and she imagined herself soaking in the energies of the items she handled.

Working in a mystical shop was both monotonous and thrilling, and sometimes Nikki experienced both sides of that in the same day. The booking of appointments, cleaning, and categorizing were repetitive, almost in a soothing way, as she settled in and learned about the business. Just as the day seemed like smooth sailing, the chime on the door would alert Nikki to someone entering the shop, and she would swear there was a famous person underneath the large sunglasses and cap. Melissa would whisk them into the back for a reading or a healing session, and Nikki marveled at what a difference her new boss made in people's lives. Nikki had seen clients walk in with stomach pain and walk out perfectly fine. Better than perfectly fine, they seemed lighter, happy.

While she was at work, Nikki could almost ignore the sorrow that had seeped into her skin, and there were times when she felt content enough to feel almost happy. Often, Destiny would cuddle up on her lap during break time or if Nikki was sitting, doing paperwork. When she purred, Nikki swore she could feel her heartrate settle into a more comfortable rhythm.

There had been no updates on her mom's murder, other than the fact that there was no DNA evidence to be found, and the prison kept terrible records on the comings and goings of staff. Theresa hadn't much luck either, as the gossip chain seemed to have been tightened. Everyone was on high alert, not knowing who to trust. A few people quit, leaving the rest of the staff tired and overworked. Even though she was nervous about being alone with colleagues that she didn't know well, Theresa reported that she didn't feel anything that seemed off. In other words, no heebie-jeebies for her. These thoughts often crept their way into Nikki's mind during the day, and she worked to push them out to deal with later. She was becoming possessive of her peace and didn't want to give it away to rumination.

Once the lunch hour rolled around, the shop was usually fairly busy, especially on the weekends. The customers ranged from the serious wiccan, looking for a specific oil or candle for spell work, to the mom who is desperate for a little peace in her household, to the teenager or college kid hoping to find something that will help them focus. On occasion, Nikki would come across a customer looking to buy weed, which they did not sell—not even to the kids who tried to slip her twenty bucks.

One afternoon, Nikki found herself alone in the shop. Melissa, who was usually there, in the back with clients, was out at a meeting and left Nikki to fend off the customers alone. It was a typical slow Tuesday, and even though the shop usually had some customers at that hour, Nikki was appreciating the quiet that surrounded her. She was already quite comfortable there, and she lit some frankincense incense. She watched the smoke rise in a steady stream, and breathed in the sweet, comforting scent.

She got lost in a blissful state of not thinking, staring at the smoke, when all of a sudden, a tiny breeze made its way through the shop. The breeze went right through the stream of incense smoke and dispersed it. Nikki watched the smoke be pushed away from her, and then look like it got sucked back in toward her, only instead of coming back to her as a billow of smoke, it came to her as a smoky face.

Nikki yelped and jumped back, heart pounding as the eyes of a smoky face stared at her for several seconds before scattering back to its original form. Within moments, the smoke was again rising toward the ceiling, as if nothing had happened. At the sound of her yell, Destiny looked up from where she had been napping in the corner of the room, behind where the face had just appeared in the smoke. The cat looked from the smoke to Nikki, like she had witnessed the entire event but was not amused. She yawned, as if Nikki's little outburst bored her, and went back to sleep.

Nikki was so freaked out that she didn't hear the chime of the door to alert her that a guest had arrived.

A voice near the register said, "Excuse me?" and Nikki just about jumped out of her skin. She laughed for a second, shaking the image from her head and thinking that she's lost it, when she realized that she was looking into the eyes of the tall man from the prison on the day that her mom was killed, the one that escorted her to see the warden. Only this time, he had an FBI jacket on, which made him less intimidating because at least he was identified as a good guy. Or so she hoped.

Startled, Nikki took a quick step back. "Holy shit, where did you come from?" she asked, peeking around him to see if maybe the door chime had fallen.

"I'm sorry, ma'am, didn't mean to startle you," he told her, while taking off his sunglasses and fixing them to the right pocket of his jacket. "I am Special Agent Higgins. We met at the prison."

If Nikki's heart wasn't pounding, she would have laughed at him—the sunglasses move and calling her ma'am were too much. "It's okay, I'm fine," she said, taking a few deep breaths. "Do you have news on my mom?"

"That is why I'm here, Ms. Ingles. While we will continue to work on this case as anything new comes up, we have exhausted our interviews, and with there being no evidence on the body, our resources are better allocated elsewhere. Unless you have any further information, of course. Now would be a suitable time to share that."

Momentarily hung up on the fact that he used the phrase *the body* instead of *your mother*, Nikki didn't speak.

"Ma'am? Do you have any further information for us? Was she having trouble with anyone? Another inmate, a guard, anyone?" the agent asked her again.

That's when Nikki saw the visit for what it was, a last-ditch effort before they called it a wrap and let a killer go free. Special Agent Higgins had nothing, and this was part of his exit strategy.

"I assure you, if I had information on my mother's murder, you would already have it," she told him. Nikki forced herself to look up at him and make direct eye contact, which neither one of them seemed to want to break.

Just when Nikki was about to look away, images of her mom's letter floating around her vision, Melissa appeared from the depths of the shop, back from her meeting. She must have entered through the back door. Her presence eased the building tension, and Nikki managed to smile at the agent. "I really don't have anything to tell you," she said. "I just want to know who killed my mom." Fresh tears ran down her cheeks, and Special Agent Higgins nodded politely.

"I'm sorry to bother you, ma'am. We both want the same thing. Please call me if anything comes up," he told her, and handed her a business card. He nodded at Melissa as he left the shop.

As Melissa watched him quietly walk out the door, she shook her head and scoffed, "They don't have a clue," she told Nikki. "And they likely never will." Melissa grabbed a tissue from the counter, which was always kept close by, and brought it to Nikki. She patted her back like a child and asked, "But you, my friend, you were holding something back."

Nikki swiped the tears off her face and tilted her head, asking, "What are you talking about?"

"Your aura is all muddy. What's going on?" Melissa took a step back and assessed the space around Nikki.

"What does that mean?" Nikki asked, looking down at her body but seeing nothing.

"Your aura?" Melissa asked, incredulously, as if everyone knew what that meant.

Nikki nodded, only a tiny bit interested in what an aura was, but glad to buy some time.

"Auras surround a person's energy field, that surrounds their physical body. Everyone has one, and the color changes depending on mood and state of mind. Not everyone can see them, but for those that can, they can be quite useful in determining what a person is going through emotionally at any given moment."

Nikki looked down at her body again, still not seeing anything. "So what color am I?" she asked.

Melissa squinted a bit, as if to see her better. "Well, normally you are a nice pink or green, meaning that you are a kind and compassionate person. Sometimes, I've seen black around you, which could mean that you are tired, which makes sense with everything you are going through. But today, you're all muddy. I can't make out any one color."

"So, what does that mean?" Nikki asked.

"It means you're hiding something. Or you were, when you were talking to agent big, or whatever his name was. What's going on?"

Nikki started to shrug her shoulders in denial, but Melissa quickly interjected, "I'm a psychic, remember? Don't tell me that nothing is happening in that brain of yours."

Crossing her arms, Nikki tried her best to hold her ground. She didn't want to tell Melissa about the letter, didn't want to think about it much less discuss it. "Well, if you're psychic, don't you already know?" Nikki forced a smile, as if she was joking but meant what she questioned.

"Haven't you learned anything in the two weeks since you started here?" Melissa asked and sighed dramatically. "There are different levels of how I get information, and various ways to get it. Sometimes, I see signs everywhere, other times a voice will pop in my head and tell me something, or I will get bits of information from another plane. Psychics don't know everything about everyone, we are in tune with energy, with the universe, with our spirit guides."

"But why don't the guides or spirits or whatever just tell you what we need to know?" Nikki asked.

"No one is meant to have all the answers, Nicole, that would defeat the whole point of going through a lifetime. We can guide you and give you insight but can't flat-out read the future or tell you what to do. Sometimes a person will ask me a question and I undoubtedly know that what I think and feel is the truth, and other times I am just as befuddled as you are. Sometimes when people are holding on to something too hard, too close, their energy field is screaming to the world to listen. To remove the burden that the body has. That's when I can hear the loudest."

"Well, I'm definitely befuddled," Nikki said, and then looked around the room, following an invisible breeze. "Did you leave a window open?" she asked Melissa, changing the subject. As Nikki wrapped her arms around herself to ward off the instant cold that she felt, she heard Destiny's bell, followed by the cat, trotting toward them.

Melissa shook her head no. "I think you're upsetting Wanda," she told Nikki. "She was never one that felt the need to explain our gifts."

"I... sorry. I just... I, wait, she's here?" Nikki looked at the space around her, suspiciously. She wondered if cats could sense the presence of a spirit and guessed that they could.

"She's often here, yes." Melissa smiled as if she were holding a great secret.

Nikki picked up on that and asked, "What are *you* holding back?"

"You first," Melissa told her, gesturing to the back room where they could sit and talk. Nikki headed in that direction and Melissa followed after locking the door to the shop and swinging the Open sign to Closed. Destiny was already in the back room, lapping up water from her dish. Once they were seated at the small round table, usually reserved for client discussions and tea breaks, Melissa looked serious and said, "You tell me what you're holding back, and I will let you speak with Wanda."

Shocked at that, Nikki started to ask what she meant, but Melissa held up her finger and said simply, "You first."

Nikki really didn't want to bring her problems to her new job, but she knew that Melissa was more than just her boss, she was becoming her friend and something of a protector. She felt more like a mother figure than anything, or what Nikki's TV version of a mother is. And so, she told her everything, about the letter that Theresa intercepted and brought to her, about the dream where she was someone else, running for her life, and about the latest dream, where the man with black eyes finally caught her.

She felt better when she finished talking, as if sharing the burden of what she knew had lifted some of it off her shoulders. Nikki noticed that Melissa's eyes were shut, and her hands were clutching on to the sides of her chair. She thought that maybe she had told her too much, maybe Melissa wasn't cut out for such drama and even danger.

Melissa opened her eyes and smiled, proving Nikki wrong. She seemed calm, as if she had been meditating all the while Nikki was talking to her. When she spoke, her voice was different. Deeper, a bit raspy. "Hello, Nicole. It's so nice to finally meet you."

11
WANDA'S PSYCHIC POWERS

Nikki laughed for a beat, thinking Melissa was messing with her, realizing quite quickly that would have been completely inappropriate timing. Nikki sat up straighter, her body vibrating with confusion and excitement. Fear. Even Destiny sat up taller and looked intrigued, like she didn't want to miss the show.

"Um, hi?" She was bewildered, knowing that something was happening but unsure what. Melissa's face smiled at her, but it was not Melissa speaking as she said, "I am Wanda. Please, do not be afraid. Melissa is perfectly safe."

Nikki didn't know how Wanda—if it was her—knew that her first thought was for Melissa's safety. Her second, third, and all thoughts after that ran in a steady stream of, *a dead person is talking to me. A dead person is talking to me. A dead person...*

"I don't have much time to speak with you," Wanda said, snapping Nikki out of her own head. "I am so glad that you have finally found us. I've been waiting to meet you for a long time."

Nikki was at a loss for what to say. She opened her mouth to speak, closed it, and tried again. Finally, she was able to get out some words, saying, "It's nice to, um, meet you, too. I don't understand how, though. And you've been waiting to meet me?" She knew that her sentence didn't make complete sense, but faced with her boss speaking in a voice that wasn't her own and that was probably a dead person, she felt proud of herself for being able to say anything.

"The *how* is easy. Melissa is a medium, and this is part of how she communicates with our clients' loved ones that have passed. It is a perfectly safe and quite effective way to speak with the dead. The *why* is a bit more complicated. I did not know it while I was alive, of course, but you are a part of my soul's journey. After I died, I learned that I was supposed to help you in this lifetime, but since we are just now meeting, it seems that our paths did not align perfectly. As they rarely do."

It was Melissa's face that smiled at that, but the expression was not her own. Nikki knew that she really was speaking with a different person. "*I* am a part of *your* soul's journey? In this *lifetime*?"

"I can see that these are new concepts for you. Unfortunately, Melissa cannot host me for long. It's exhausting for her. You will both need to rest. You have a long journey ahead of you. There is a storm brewing, Nicole. You are in danger."

Right away Nikki thought of her mom. "Does this have anything to do with my mom? Is she still *around*?" she asked, thinking of the warning she had received after the murder, wondering if her mom was nearby.

"It has nothing and everything to do with her. Your mother is close, yes, but she is healing. I cannot say too much, but you need to forgive, Nicole. You need to heal your past, not just your past in this lifetime but in your previous life. If you can learn to forgive, you might avoid repeating this cycle in future lives."

"What do you mean, repeat this cycle in future lives? I'm worried about *this* life," Nikki was surprised at how quick she was to accept the idea of reincarnation. Then again, she was talking to a spirit named Wanda, through her new boss. It's easy to stretch your beliefs when the truth is right in your face.

Melissa's head shook sadly, while Wanda's voice said, "I fear it may be too late, Nicole. Sometimes we must accept our fate. This entire lifetime was created for you to repent. There are others around you that feel different, and have been working hard to save you."

"My mom? Was she trying to save me?" Nikki asked, tears forming in her eyes.

"Your mother was here to support you," Wanda explained. "Her soul had some issues to work out and she was able to do that while teaching you something about resilience. Your mother's hardships will directly help you in your journey of forgiveness."

Nikki did not want to forgive. She wanted to find whoever had killed her mom and make them pay for what they had done. She wanted to find them and hurt them. Looking directly into Melissa's eyes was spooky when in this state, as the whites stood out so that she looked perpetually surprised, but Nikki did it anyway. She wanted to make sure Wanda knew she meant business as she said, "Maybe my life is not about forgiveness. Maybe it is about revenge."

Wanda did not break that eye contact as she warned Nikki one last time, "Then you will only find another creative way to suffer in your next life. The revenge you seek is not against the person who killed your mom but on yourself. And I'm telling you right now, you need to heal that wound, or it is not only your life, right here and now, that is on the line, but all your future lives, as well."

Chills of truth swirled around Nikki's consciousness. She fell silent. Not knowing what Wanda was talking about was frustrating, but she could feel an understanding in the nape of her neck, and a spot in the center of her forehead began to tingle. She put her hand there, expecting to feel something, but it was only skin. "That is your third eye, Nicole. It's waking up," Wanda explained, looking slightly satisfied. "I pray that you can hear me through all of the doubt clouding your vision."

Nikki was about to ask what she meant by that, but she suddenly felt a shift in the room. A slight breeze blew by her as Melissa's body relaxed into the chair, eyes closing as if in a deep slumber.

A mix of feelings came over Nikki. She was both astounded that she had spoken with a spirit and disheartened that she still didn't have more solid information. Destiny seemed to know what was needed, and she jumped into her lap, purring as if were her job to settle Nikki down.

Melissa opened her eyes and looked at Nikki. Propping up her chin on her hands, she asked, "So, what did I miss?"

12
LOST

Nikki spent the next several days attempting to decode what Wanda had told her. Finding as much information as she could about past lives became an obsession for her. It seemed like the more she learned, the more confused she was, since there is so much conflicting information in the world about reincarnation. And even if one source was supporting the reincarnation theory, it wasn't necessarily supporting the whole *forgive yourself now or suffer later* theory. Especially because for the life of her, Nikki couldn't figure out what she was forgiving herself for. It's not as if she *killed* someone, for God's sake. Sure, she had done some pretty shitty stuff but also some shitty things were done *to* her, so she felt like karma was doing a good job at balancing out her life. Well, this life, anyway. And didn't people get a blank slate when they die?

The questions were driving her crazy, and so was Melissa's vague answers to her endless follow-up questions after her strange conversation with Wanda. Melissa seemed unfazed by it all, and when they were together at the shop, it almost seemed like she was avoiding Nikki.

Nikki felt like Melissa ran hot or cold. One day, she would seem like her best friend and confidant, and the next day it seemed like Melissa was skirting around Nikki as if it was her life's mission. Plus, it felt like she knew more about Nikki's current life, and past life, than Nikki did, but she wasn't offering any information. Frustrated and needing some answers—about anything—Nikki decided to ask Theresa to meet her after work. She wished that she could meet up for a drink, but Ken warned Nikki (over and over and over again) about the dangers of drinking when she was still in recovery. When she asked him when her recovery would be over and she could resume a normal life, Ken laughed that halfhearted laugh and told her, "Maybe in your next life."

That shocked Nikki and she was instantly suspicious as to why he would use that phrase, but when Ken explained that drinking alcohol can trigger past traumatic experiences, and that someone with a history of drug abuse can be very easily triggered, she figured that he was just protecting her. Even thinking of that conversation made Nikki want a drink, so she texted Theresa and asked if maybe she would like to go for a hike together.

Moments after hitting send she received a text back from Theresa, who said she would *love* to go on a hike. Nikki laughed, wondering if Theresa really just loved to hike, or if she, like herself, would rather go on a bender but decided to jump at the more socially acceptable method of getting some feel-good energy going.

·   ·   ·   ·   ·

Nikki was not the best planner, and both she and Theresa realized about an hour into the hike that they were going to have to hurry up or find a shortcut to be out of the woods by the time it got dark. The two were chatting easily about life while they made their way up and down the rolling expanse of woods. The tree cover was thick, so the woods were darker than either of them liked but having the company of each other encouraged them to push their comfort zone.

Nikki thought about asking Theresa what she knew about past lives and reincarnation but decided that might be weird on their first outing together. Plus, Theresa had become a part of Nikki's life in such a bizarre way—through her mom's letter, really—that Nikki felt a little pushy about making their new friendship any weirder so soon. So, they kept the conversation light, even as the darkness grew around them.

As far back as Nikki could remember, she had had an aversion for the hour or so surrounding dusk.

When the sun begins to set and one can feel the subtle shift in the temperature, and the sky darkens as slow as time can move, a sadness almost always overcomes her. It is not something she had ever been able to put into words, but on that hike, there was a noticeable shift in her energy.

"Are you all right?" Theresa asked, stumbling over some downed branches to catch up. "You got awful quiet all of a sudden." Theresa knew that Nikki was still processing what had happened to her mom, which was difficult since they had no answers, and she worried about her. In fact, she had already been on her mind when she got the surprise text asking if she wanted to go on a hike.

Nikki was not feeling all right. She knew the familiar feeling of sadness creeping in, but also knowing that there was no way to explain this she tried to shake it off and keep moving. "Oh, I'm okay, just lost in my own thoughts, I guess," she said, and then, "hang on."

Theresa stopped in her tracks and asked, "What's wrong?"

Nikki stopped too and looked all around them. There was still plenty of light, but the shadows were growing longer. They hadn't hiked that far, maybe a mile or so from where they had left Theresa's car, but Nikki was looking at a stream that she didn't remember seeing on their way up.

"I don't remember seeing that stream on our way in," Nikki said, pointing just a few yards to their left. "Did I miss it?"

Theresa, hands on her hips, looked all around her. She thought about it, opened her mouth to speak, closed it, and did another three-sixty all around her. "You know," she finally answered, "if you missed it then so did I. In fact, none of this looks familiar."

They must have been walking faster than they thought, because all Nikki could hear when she looked around was their heavy breathing. She laughed and looked to Theresa while she said, "I guess I'm more out of shape than I realized." Nikki stopped laughing as she saw the look on Theresa's face. It wasn't fear but total confusion. "What is it?" she asked her, following her gaze to a little patch of downed trees.

Theresa shook her head and answered, "I don't know, exactly. I'm getting a weird sense of déjà vu."

Nikki didn't even realize that her feet were carrying her to where Theresa was looking. "That's weird. Like, really weird," she said, peering closer into the thick fallen branches. "I feel like I've been here. Or seen this place? But I have definitely never been here before."

"Me either," Theresa said, following Nikki closer to the trees. "But it reminds me of a dream I had."

The dream. It all came back to Nikki, and she felt dizzy. She remembered her nightmare, being chased, hunted. Hiding in the thick brush of fallen trees. Hearing that voice calling for her but not her, exactly.

Nikki realized that Theresa was by her side, and she told her about the dream. About running and hearing the crunching of the leaves behind her. And the voice, calling for her.

"Julietta," Theresa whispered, shocked.

Nikki spun to face Theresa, fear crawling its way up her spine, hugging her bones, and tightening her chest. "What did you just say?" she asked, fighting to control a tremble that was trying to work its way out of her.

Theresa shook her head, as if trying to clear it. "I don't know, exactly. I had the strangest nightmare the other night, and right before I woke up, I heard the name Julietta. This place reminds me of my dream. More than reminds me—I feel like I was just right here."

"And in this dream," Nikki asked her, slowing her breath. "Did you happen to be chasing me?"

"Not you, someone else. And I wasn't chasing, but watching, like from a distance. Almost like I was above it all."

"Well, holy shit on a stick," Nikki said, her childhood curses flowing out as if she was a little kid again. "I had the same dream, same place, only *I* was the one being chased. It's like you saw my dream."

The two women stood in that spot for what felt like minutes, the sun dipping a little lower with each passing second. They just stared at each other, a little wary but mostly confused.

Finally, Theresa broke the silence and said, "Well, that's freaking weird," and forced out a laugh.

It sounded out of place but made Nikki smile. She took a deep breath in. Out. When she spoke, the fear had mostly subsided. "I don't know what's happening here, but my life has gone from bad to okay to fucked-up in a matter of weeks. I feel like I'm on an out-of-control Ferris wheel. I feel..." Nikki paused and walked to the spot where she had hidden in her dream. She picked up the soil as if to inspect it, but she was really just feeling it to make sure it was real and continued her thought, looked from the soil running through her hands to Theresa and continued, "lost."

Theresa smiled and walked over to Nikki, putting her hand on her shoulder. It was an odd gesture for her, but she felt the need to offer comfort. "I hear that," she told Nikki. "My life is taking a pretty strange turn, as well. And technically," she said, pointing into the darkening woods. "We are lost. Let's get out of here. I don't think I can handle all of this in the dark."

Together they made their way down the mountain and found themselves about a quarter mile away from where Theresa parked her car. While they walked down the back road, glad that they had gotten out of the woods but still hurrying to beat the oncoming nightfall, they stayed close to each other.

Every few feet, one of them would cast a glance over their shoulder, into the woods, never seeing anything but feeling unsettled anyway.

They heard a car approaching and although neither said a word, they both ducked into the trees on the side of the road. As the car passed them, they let out a collective sigh and laughed at themselves.

"Paranoid, perhaps?" Nikki said, glad that she now saw Theresa's car as they turned a corner.

The driver of the car did not see the two women walking down the side of the road, didn't see them duck into the tree line as he passed. He did, however, feel a warm shudder run through his body. As Hadeon rolled down his window, he sniffed the air, feeling like a wild animal. He drove a few more yards and pulled off on the side of the road. He felt like he was close to something, but he didn't know what. It seemed like he was operating lately on pure instinct, not entirely in control of his body or senses. He didn't care—the feeling made him happy.

As he sat in his car on the side of the road, he thought about the woman he had killed in the prison. He didn't know why he had killed her—it just seemed like what he had to do. She did not fit the criteria of who he had been subconsciously looking for, but she came close enough. All part of this new instinct that he was working with. Ever since he had that brief interaction with the scrawny young woman that he spoke to in the prison lobby, his senses were heightened. His subconscious began to rise into his conscious thought, and all he knew was that she brought something primal out of him. Not feeling any remorse, he sniffed the air again, howled like a wolf, and drove off into the night.

13
SECRETS

The day after the hike with Theresa, Nikki got to work early so she could talk to Melissa about it. She really needed some answers and hoped that Melissa would be willing to share some insights with her.

The door was already unlocked, and the bells jingled as Nikki pushed her way inside. The familiar scent of incense and oils got her attention right away, and she inhaled, feeling her heart settle.

Destiny was already lounging on the counter, which meant that Melissa was in early, as well, as both she and the cat lived upstairs in the apartment above the shop and came to work together.

Nikki had planned on grabbing Melissa's ear first thing, before she got busy, but realized that she wasn't as early as she thought when she heard a man's voice in the back room. Figuring she may as well open the register and set up for the day, she walked closer to the back of the shop, and realized that she knew the voice. It was unmistakably Ken's voice, and while she couldn't make out exactly what they were saying, it sounded like they were having an argument.

She couldn't help herself, and as Nikki tiptoed closer to the door, the voices stopped. From the other side of the door, Melissa greeted Nikki, "Good morning, Nicole. You may as well come in."

Nikki opened the door and was surprised but not surprised to find Ken and Melissa sitting at the little round table together, drinking coffee.

"How did you know I was there?" Nikki asked, squinting her eyes at the pair of them, feeling annoyed that they didn't even look uncomfortable to be caught chatting it up this early in the morning. It's not like they were friends or really even know each other, besides meeting at her mom's funeral. *Were they secretly seeing each other?* Nikki wondered, not sure she could handle any more secrets.

"Oh, for Pete's sake," Melissa said, snapping her out of her thoughts. "You look like you just busted your parents having sex. I knew you were there because not only am I psychic, but you are also loud. And Ken came here to see you. I just had the good fortune to beat you to this delicious treat." Melissa held up the cup and Nikki saw that it came from her favorite coffee shop.

"Oh," was all she could think of saying. "It sounded like someone was arguing," she said, looking at Ken, realizing that he hadn't even greeted her.

"Not arguing," Melissa told her, getting up to pull out a chair for Nikki. She gestured for her to sit, and confessed, "Just a little disagreement."

That sounded fishy to Nikki. "Disagreement? Over what, coffee flavors?"

Melissa laughed, but Nikki noticed the direct eye contact she made with Ken.

Ken, who had been silent up until that point, smiled at Nikki and asked her, "Do you ever have the feeling that you are so close to all of the answers you seek, but forces just keep getting in your way of figuring things out?"

"Yeah, I do," Nikki answered quickly. "Forces, murders, mediums," she said, looking to Melissa. "I feel that way all the time. I work for a psychic who knows more about me than I do, yet all I do is ask questions that I do not have answers for. It was like this shop stalked me until I came here, and once it got me, that fountain of mystery stopped flowing."

"All right, Nicole," Melissa said, patting her on the hand like a grandmother would. "I wouldn't say stopped. We are just..." she paused and at that exact moment, the bells over the door jingled, as if someone were entering. "We are just trying to protect you."

"Protect me from what?" Nikki asked, still confused as to how Ken and Melissa had anything to do with each other, nevertheless their role in her safety. She started to get up from the table, to see to the customer that must have entered.

Melissa stopped her from getting up, saying, "It's not a customer, Nikki. The door did not open."

"But it..." Nikki stopped speaking as a cool chill entered the room—just like that, the room didn't get cooler, the coolness came in the door. "Ah, Wanda?" she guessed.

Ken's eyes got wider. *Clearly*, Nikki thought, *he is out of his element here.* She tried to act as if this was something she was used to, but the truth was, Wanda kind of freaked her out, and she was much happier at work when she didn't feel any spirity feelings around.

Nikki waited for something to happen, looking at Melissa to see if her eyes were rolling, or if perhaps a windstorm would kick up. Seconds ticked by. Nothing.

Impatient, she asked Ken, "Hang on, what answers are you looking for? I thought you were just here to bring me coffee."

Ken sighed. "Yes," he said, shaking his head just a bit. "And no. I am tired of keeping secrets from you, tired of going from being the one with the answers to being the one with the questions, and tired of trying to keep you safe when I do not know where the danger is." He shrugged his shoulders and looked at Melissa. To her he said, "I think it's time."

Melissa shook her head no. "She's not ready, Ken. She's still grieving. She—"

Nikki cut her off, pleading with them, "Please, just tell me what the hell is going on here. I will always be grieving, that won't go away. I-I don't think I can move on without knowing why I am scared all the time. I want to know who killed my mom, I want to know why I'm having nightmares that other people are also having, I want to know what Wanda meant when she said I must forgive myself when I really can't remember doing anything to anyone besides myself. Please." She was out of words and felt comfort when she felt an unseen hand on her back.

Nikki looked to Melissa, who was nodding as if someone were speaking to her. She saw Nikki notice and asked her, "Have you ever heard of past life regression hypnosis?"

That sounded scary to Nikki. "Uh, no. Can't you just tell me what you know?"

Melissa shook her head and said, "Some things can't be told, Nicole. Some things you need to remember for yourself. I just hope you are strong enough to handle it."

"Of course, she is," Ken interjected. He reached across the table and took Nikki's hand. He closed his eyes and breathed deep, as if he were preparing himself for something painful. Nikki was confused, as this was her life she would be remembering. "Just remember, Nikki, I am right here."

"Ooookay," Nikki told him, feeling a little weird about his reaction but also knowing, from a place inside her that she was just learning existed, that he was there for her with only good intentions. Still, she had to wonder about his motivations, and stated,

"But I'm kind of surprised that you would be into this, you know, with you being so into the Bible and all."

Ken nodded and looked like he was really contemplating her statement. Rather than answer directly, he quoted the Bible, a passage from Luke 8:17. "For nothing is hidden that will not become evident, nor anything secret that will not be known and come to light."

"Um, Ken, you know I don't speak Bible verse," Nikki told him, pulling her hand away from his and sitting up taller in her chair.

Ken smiled. "It just means that secrets cannot stay hidden forever," he explained, making eye contact with Melissa.

As if on cue, Melissa stretched her arms out in a grand gesture and said to Nikki, "Nicole, are you ready to go back in time?"

Nikki was all nerves but said, "Yes ma'am," and put on the bravest smile that she could.

"That's good," Melissa said, but instead of starting the session she pointed at the door. "But first, go lock the door. Secrets should be known, but they do not need to be shared with the public."

As Nikki got up to lock the door, she felt that chill in the air again and knew it was Wanda. Apparently, she didn't want to miss the show any more than Ken did. She quickly locked the door and turned the sign to Closed, and when Nikki got back to the table to sit down, she noticed Destiny, who had jumped up on her chair and was patiently waiting for her to get back and give her some love.

"Does she give this much support to all of your clients?" Nikki asked Melissa, impressed by how intuitive the cat was.

Melissa smiled and reached across the table to pat Destiny's head when Nikki sat down. "Destiny has a special gift for knowing when she is needed," she told Nikki. "Are you ready to get started?"

Nikki held Destiny closer, as if she could shield her from what was to come. "I'm ready," she said, letting her feline friend work her magic to calm her quick beating heart, and relax.

14
THE CONTRACT

Melissa turned off the lights and wound up her old metronome to start the hypnosis session. Nikki, desperate for answers, was easy to coax into a relaxed enough state to walk back through time.

Nikki laughed as she recalled people from her past, was delighted to see her children, cried as she remembered how they died. Every time that Nikki recalled a past life, she quickly felt the emotions of remembering, and then leapt ahead to another life, satisfied with how each life was complete.

Melissa made eye contact with Ken as Nikki remembered her life as Julie. Nikki was happy to have found her soul mate once again. She and James were the happiest that they had been together when tragedy struck just one week after their second wedding anniversary. They had decided to go on a trip to celebrate, and Julie took off work to pack. They were supposed to leave for a 5 p.m. flight, but James never showed up. Julie knew within an hour of his not arriving home that something was wrong, and she called the local hospital. Sure enough, James was there. At first Julie was relieved but the relief soon ended when the emergency room doctor took her call, and told her the heartbreaking news that James had a sudden brain aneurysm, and died.

Sadly, that was not the worst part of that life for Nikki to remember. When she recalled the accident, and the promise that James made to her, she became overwrought with emotion, and ended the session abruptly.

Nikki quietly put the cat down, left the room, and burst through the door of Wanda's Psychic Powers, causing the door chimes to jingle incessantly. She left the shop without saying goodbye and ran down the street, toward her apartment. All the while, the constant *tick tick tick* of the metronome played in her ears.

She couldn't think, couldn't even fathom what she had just learned, and she tried to push it from her mind. "No, no, no no no no no no," she repeated, only barely registering that she had uttered those nos before. In her past.

Nikki got to her apartment building and took the stairs two at a time. She didn't know why she was in such a hurry to get there, other than the ability to shut her door, lock it, and turn the rest of the world away. She finally reached the landing and made a hard left, practically sprinting toward what she now called home.

Just steps away from her door, Nikki saw something on the ground. She felt that time stilled as she slowed from a run to a walk, stopping in front of a child's size sneaker. It was a bright blue Ked, and it was splattered with red. Blood.

Slowly, Nikki, who was bent over the shoe, reached out and picked it up. The blood was wet and sticky, and Nikki could smell a mix of something metallic with an old-sneaker scent. She dropped the sneaker and screamed, heart pounding so loud she barely heard her own yell.

"Hey, Nicole, are you all right?" It was Mr. McKinney from two doors down, typical old neighbor that hears everything. That's what Nikki joked about him to Ken when she first moved in—she'd called him the resident old nosy neighbor.

She turned to face Mr. McKinney and, breathlessly told him, "I'm not sure. There's this shoe here and it's all bloody." She pointed behind her to the shoe but couldn't bring herself to look at it.

"Ah, Nicole, sweetheart, there is nothing there," Mr. McKinney told her, looking worried in his pajamas. Then he asked, "Do you need me to walk you inside?"

Nikki turned to look at the spot in front of her door, and Mr. McKinney was right, there was nothing there. No shoe. No blood. No scent.

"Um. Sorry, Mr. McKinney. I must have seen a shadow or something," Nikki told him, and with shaking hands, pulled her key out of her front pocket. "Everything is fine."

"Yeah, um-hm. Fine. You're not using again are you, Nicole?"

Nosy is right. Nikki did her best to smile at him and assured him that she was not on drugs. "I've just been working a lot. Kind of jumpy," she said, and pushed her door open.

Nikki didn't say goodbye and instead ducked into her apartment and shut the door, the refuge that she had been seeking finally found. That feeling of peace didn't last long as Nikki leaned on the door. She closed her eyes and let her head hit the door behind her, and when it did, it made a little knocking sound.

Knocking sound. A knock sounded like a thump, which sounded like Nikki, in a life that she was only just remembering, running over a little boy with her car.

"Oh my God," she whispered. She hadn't wanted to believe any of what she saw as Melissa walked her through the past life hypnosis session. But it was all true, she knew it just as she knew that the little boy's sneaker was a bright blue Ked, and that he lost it when she hit him. She saw the entire accident and felt herself tremble as she relived her death. Watched again as little Kenny was lifted by his dad and carried off to what she always thought of as the healing place. The wave, the smile, the facial features—all of them familiar in this life. Kenny was Ken, her savior, also her victim.

"Oh my God," again she whispered as fact upon fact piled on her shoulders. She felt their weight and sank to the floor. "Kenny is Ken, I am Julie. I am Julietta and..."

Nikki began to remember pieces of this life combined with her past life, remembered the nightmare where she was being chased. The voice, calling, "Juliet-ta" and finally finding her.

The voice. James. Her soul mate. Nikki closed her eyes as she thought of James, trying to save her from her grief after the accident. She remembered her other lives, too. Children. Illness. Death. It was too much for her and she covered her ears with her hands, trying unsuccessfully to drown out the voices that were haunting her from her past.

Tears flowed as Nikki again remembered the accident. She, as Julie, had been so sad after her husband died and had turned to alcohol for comfort. *Not too far of a stretch,* Nikki thought, thinking of all the times in her current life that she turned to alcohol or drugs for comfort. Making herself focus on the memory, she pictured the day that she died in that life, hungover and late for work. Before her husband died, she had loved her job. Loved the kids, everything about teaching them. But once he passed, she was totally alone in the world and depressed. And that, she knew, was no excuse for being so careless. All the pain she experienced from loss in that lifetime meant nothing to her as she imagined little Kenny as he went under her car. The pain and fear he must have felt.

She wanted to talk to Ken, to say how sorry she was, but she didn't know how she could ever face him again. Why on Earth was he helping her now? And James, her soul mate. What had she done?

There was a contract made, she remembered. He had promised to kill her. Not only kill her but make her suffer. Well, her life certainly made sense now. "How could I do that to him?" she asked the empty room. "I deserve whatever I'm getting, but he does not."

Nikki got up off the floor and went into the bathroom, feeling panicked but purposeful. She blew her nose and washed her face. Feeling only slightly better, she peered at her face in the mirror. "I will make this right," she told her reflection. "I don't know how, but if a contract was made there must be a way to break it. I'll kill myself if I have to. Then no one will have to kill me..."

She stopped talking midsentence, as one more piece of the puzzle clicked into place somewhere in her brain. "My mom," she told the reflection in the mirror, who started to cry again, big, fast tears dripping onto the sink. "This is my fault. He must have been looking for me and found her."

Was it a warning? Was it part of the plan to make her suffer? Or was it just a crapshoot; some guy was hunting some girl for reasons he maybe didn't even know and stumbled upon an older and slightly more beat-up version of—

"Wait." Nikki stopped the stream of thoughts. "The letter."

Nikki ran to her bed and stuck her hand between the mattress and box spring. She pulled out the letter that her mom wrote to her, and Theresa found and delivered. She read it again: He sniffed me— like, actually sniffed me like a dog—and said that he's been looking for me for a long time. I have never seen this guy in my life, I swear. I tried to flirt with him, hoping that he was looking to get lucky and in turn give me some perks, but he grabbed my wrist and told me that he'd see me again soon.

Nikki had figured that whoever this person was, and she assumed it was the guy who had killed her mom, was demented and trying to scare her. Or maybe he was some nut who actually thought that her mom was Nikki and had some grudge. Of all the drug dealers, pimps, and customers that Nikki knew, she figured that a handful of them must not be above killing a lowly inmate. But this truth, the knowledge that this was most likely James and that he had killed her mom thinking it might be Nikki—or close enough to Nikki to satisfy some urge—that was too much for her to bear.

"I'm so sorry, Mom," she whispered, crinkling up the letter and shoving it back under the mattress. Who else would James hurt, in order to hurt Nikki? Maybe it wasn't about killing her yet, maybe it was about making her suffer, as promised. She remembered the exact moment that he made that promise to her, how he had doomed himself to help her heal. The damage that he was doing to his own soul, killing an innocent person, was devastating to Nikki.

Still confused and overwhelmed with memories, Nikki's head was starting to clear. She didn't know how to fix the mess she had created, but she knew that she had to find James, and somehow free him from the promise that he made to her. She just hoped that neither of them had to die to make things right.

15
GOLDEN GLOBES

Nikki was pacing her apartment, trying to figure out where to find James. The trouble was, she had no idea where to look. She couldn't get into the one place where she knew he had been. The prison where her mom had been killed was not about to let her start poking around with questions, and other than an odd, creepy sensation now and then, she had no idea if she had ever even laid eyes on him.

She decided to call Theresa, to find out if there'd been any talk at all among the staff about someone who didn't fit in, seemed weird or violent, or if anyone had theories of their own that they had shared now that the feds were gone.

Theresa picked up on the first ring, and she was breathless. "Hello?" she answered as if she hadn't even seen who was calling, as if she was preoccupied and didn't even look.

"Hey Theresa, it's Nikki. Everything okay?"

"Oh my God. Nikki," Theresa said, and then she started to cry. "I've been so freaked out and had my phone out to call for help, but I didn't know who to call. Or what to say, or—oh shit."

"What's the matter? Where are you?" Nikki asked.

"I'm in the woods. Where we went hiking," Theresa told her, sniffling her words out.

Nikki was confused and asked, "You're hiking? Are you lost?"

"I'm not sure. I had that dream again—the one about the woods—only this time, I was the one being chased. I was running for so long, from the woods to my house, but when I got to my house, I was already home, and I was the one who was doing the chasing." Theresa paused, and Nikki could hear her pacing in circles, could imagine the leaves kicking up around her ankles. She continued, but quicker, saying, "I woke up in a panic and drove right here. I don't know why exactly—to look for answers maybe? But obviously all I've found is myself lost in the woods. Again. I got spooked about a half hour ago and I can't find my way out."

Theresa sounded like she was panicking, and Nikki didn't blame her. "Stay calm, it will be okay. I'll come and find you," she told her.

"Really?" Theresa asked, clearly relieved. "Oh my God. Thank you."

"Well," Nikki told her. "Don't thank me until I've found you. Remember what happened last time we went hiking."

Nikki meant to lighten the mood but knew she did not. As she hung up the phone, she also knew that she needed help, because she just offered hers and she did not own a car and didn't know of any bus routes that went near where Theresa was.

She needed help, and the only two people she felt close enough to ask were Melissa and Ken. Neither seemed like the best option at the moment, seeing how she ran out on them, but also knowing that she would have to go back to work sooner rather than later, Nikki opted to call Melissa.

Fifteen minutes later, Nikki was in Melissa's car, navigating where to go.

"I still don't understand how you were able to get to me so fast." Nikki was questioning Melissa, always thinking that she knew something that she wasn't sharing.

Melissa only smiled and explained, with the patience a teacher might give a child, and said, "I cannot see into the future, Nicole. This gift does not work like that. I can, however, sense when someone I care about is in danger, or needs my help."

"What does it feel like?" Nikki asked.

"Well, it depends. I have learned so much from Wanda, and my senses are changing all the time. Sometimes it's like someone is yelling right in my face to take action. And other times, it's just a tingle, maybe a twinge right where my third eye is, and someone will come to mind. Occasionally, a spirit will talk to me directly, but that is unusual. Even though the spirits and our guides want to help us, it's still important to them that we figure things out for ourselves."

Nikki was satisfied with that answer, for the moment, as she was still reeling from the information she had learned about her past life. And about Ken.

Melissa seemed to read her mind, and told her, "I'm here whenever you want to talk about it."

"I just can't believe that I killed Ken. I mean, it's crazy. And I have a soul mate out there who loved me so much he is willing to kill me just so I feel better. It's overwhelming," Nikki admitted.

Melissa nodded her head. "I know," she said, "it's a lot for all of us to take in."

"All of?" Nikki started to ask, but they came upon Theresa's car, and Melissa pulled behind it and shut off the engine.

They got out and Nikki somehow led them, on instinct, close to the spot both she and Theresa recognized from their oddly similar nightmares.

"Theresa? Theresa!" Nikki called out, but there was no sign of her. They walked around the woods for a while, splitting up but never out of earshot from one another, and after about twenty minutes, Nikki finally had the bright idea to call her cell.

Nikki could hear the phone ringing in her ear and about ten feet from where she stood. "What the...?" she said aloud, searching for the ringing sound on the ground. The call went to voice mail but not before Nikki spotted Theresa's cell phone at the base of a tree. Little tingles of fear crept all over her body, and for a moment she couldn't speak, couldn't call to Melissa for help.

Thankfully, that moment passed, and she yelled to Melissa, who was already loudly making her way to Nikki, stepping on branches in no effort to be quiet. Nikki held up the phone and, bewildered, handed it to Melissa.

"Well, I didn't find Theresa, but I did find her phone," Nikki said. She was getting worried, and she could tell by the look on Melissa's face that she was, too.

Melissa took the phone and studied it, as if it held some clues.

Nikki was wondering what she was doing but kept her questions to herself as Melissa closed her eyes and took a deep breath. Eyes still closed, she turned her head as if looking through the forest, peering although she could not see. Although that was not entirely true and Nikki knew it, as Melissa could sense as well as she could see with her eyes, and without saying a word, opened her eyes and began walking in the opposite direction that they came from.

Silently, Nikki followed her through the trees, over stumps, sidestepping some very large ferns, until about forty yards later, Melissa stopped walking. She broke the silence, Nikki realized, right where she and Theresa had dreamed about, in the thick patch of fallen trees.

Melissa knelt right out of Nikki's sight, and softly said, "I've found her."

Nikki jogged the last few feet, thinking the worst, not daring to imagine how she would find her friend, and was relieved to find her sitting up and wiping tears from her face.

Melissa sat right on the ground next to Theresa and put her arm around her. She asked her, "What's going on? Are you all right?"

Theresa shook her head and said, "I don't know. I'm okay, I guess. After I hung up with Nikki earlier, I was pretty sure that someone was following me. I dropped my phone but was too scared to go back for it. I ran in circles for a bit. I'm pretty sure I lost him."

"Him?" Nikki asked, looking around the woods. It was beginning to get dark, and having a strong sense of déjà vu, Nikki wanted to get out of there. "Did you see him? Do you know who it is? Was he just, like, lurking around the woods?"

Theresa wiped her eyes one last time and started to stand. Melissa jumped up to lend a hand as Theresa gratefully took it, telling Nikki, "I only got a quick glimpse of him. I was hiking around, not sure what I was even doing there, about to head back to the car when I rolled my ankle and stumbled. I sat down for a minute and took my sneaker off. I heard some branches break over toward the stream, and when I looked up, there was a guy standing there, just staring at me. He scared the crap out of me, and I yelled out, and then tried to laugh it off and called to him. 'Hello?' I yelled, but he didn't make a move, he just stood there watching me. I was very aware that I was all alone in the woods with this weirdo, so I put my shoe back on, looking down at it for just a few seconds. When I looked back up, he was gone."

Chills circled Nikki again, this time settling on that space on her forehead where she learned her third eye was. She still didn't understand any of that but figured it had something to do with intuition. *Could he still be close?* she wondered.

"He didn't say anything?" Nikki asked Theresa, all three of them still looking over their shoulders and around each other.

"Not a word. All he did was stare, and even though he was a bit away, it felt like we were making direct eye contact. Of course, he had freaky eyes—almost a gold color—contacts maybe? That made it even creepier."

Nikki's breath hitched in her chest.

"What is it?" Melissa asked her. "You look like you've just seen a ghost."

"Not a ghost," Nikki said, remembering the wild amber eyes that the man outside the prison had. "I literally bumped into some guard at the prison once. He gave me the creeps, and he had eyes so amber, they looked gold."

"I don't remember seeing a guard with eyes like that," Theresa said, thinking back. "About how long ago was this?"

Nikki's own eyes went large as she remembered. "It was right before my mom was killed."

Oh, Nikki thought, and *holy shit*. "That must be the guy who killed my mom. I freaking talked to him." With fresh tears, she asked Melissa, "Is that James? He didn't act like he knew me. I don't understand."

Melissa took Nikki's hand and told her, "If that is the person who killed your mom, and if that person is the soul's manifestation of James, he wouldn't know you. Just like you are not Julie, you are an individual in this life, he is only operating on some preprogrammed instinct. And those instincts are fuzzy," she explained.

Confused, Nikki asked, "But in my mom's letter, she said that a guard sniffed her like a dog. He asked about my birthday. How could that be possible that he did not recognize me at all? And how is it that I wanted to find him, but instead he finds Theresa?"

"Well, it could be that seeing you triggered some deep memory for his soul's journey. It's hard to really say," Melissa was explaining this, but also looking around wildly. "I think we should get out of here before we can't find our way in the dark," she said.

"But—" Nikki started, desperately wanting her questions answered.

Melissa cut her off. "There will be time for questions, Nicole, but we must find safety first. I have questions of my own. For you, Theresa," she said, nodding toward Theresa, "and for you, too, Nicole.

You shouldn't be looking for this man at all. You know he wants to kill you."

"But I thought that if I just found him and explained everything, I could save him from killing me and ruining his life. Or lives, or something," Nikki said, defending herself.

Melissa shook her head and told Nikki, "This man is dangerous. You can't just talk sense into a person who has no idea why they are acting as they are. He could have been killing people all his life to work up to this, we don't know. And if he has, then you are in danger, and so are we, by walking around here, especially in the dark. It's time to use our heads, ladies," she told them, leading the way back to the cars.

Nikki and Theresa both followed, feeling a little chastised. But knowing she was right, they kept quiet. Nikki felt like there were eyes everywhere, little golden globes that could steal her soul. She wondered if this was James, and if he was hunting her as she was looking for him? And if so, why look here? Why would he find Theresa and not her?

Shuddering, Nikki realized she was a little jealous, which made her feel sick. This man killed her mom and wanted to kill her. So what if he is her soul mate? She had to get a grip, she knew, and as they found the safety of the cars, Nikki peered one last time into the woods behind her, searching for those golden eyes.

16
THE PACT

At Melissa's request, the three of them headed back to Wanda's Psychic Powers to talk. She and Nikki rode in silence while Theresa followed in her car, and Nikki noticed that every so often, Melissa would glance in her rearview mirror, as if she were checking to see that Theresa was still behind them.

"What, you think that she's going to bail?" Nikki asked, breaking the quiet, wondering what Melissa could be thinking.

"No," Melissa answered, checking behind them yet again. "I'm just going over all of this in my mind, and I simply cannot figure out where Theresa comes into play here. What am I missing? What does Theresa have to do with all of this?"

Nikki told her the story about how it was Theresa who found the letter that her mom had written to her before she died, which Melissa already knew of but wanted to hear about again anyway. Nikki also told her about the dream that they shared, and how they both realized that they were in the location of the dream when they went hiking.

"So, you weren't friends before all of this started happening?" Melissa asked.

"Um, no, not really. She was at the prison a lot, working at the check-in desk. She was always kind to me and never seemed to judge me or my mom," Nikki told her. And then she asked, "Why? You don't think she is *bad*, do you?"

Melissa smiled and looked over to Nikki, warmth returning to her features. "No, I quite like Theresa," she said. "I just can't seem to get a good read on her."

"Read on her?" Nikki asked.

"Yes, when I try to look into anything about her— her aura, her psychic connections, anything—I feel a sort of push back. I've experienced this before, sometimes people are subconsciously very protective of psychic energies poking around."

They were quiet for a few minutes and then Nikki asked, "How is it possible that Theresa and I had nearly the same dream, but from a different perspective?"

Melissa shrugged and shook her head, saying, "I'm not sure. That's one of the things I can't get a read on. It could just be that you are connected through the trauma of your mom. I'm sure that it shook her up to find that letter and bring it to you. You may have developed a psychic connection with her."

Nikki added, "True, she was pretty upset when she brought the letter to me. Scared, I think. I trust her, though, if that means anything."

"It does. I'm sure that trust doesn't come easy for you," Melissa said, and she was right.

"Honestly, I just feel so lucky that I have a circle of people who are looking out for me. Although it seems crazy and unfair that it was Ken who saved me and led me to this different sort of life. I can't believe that I killed him," Nikki said, fighting back tears. She had never cried so much in her entire life. It felt like she was not only mourning her mom, but her dad again, and then who she was in her past lives. And of course, what she had James do for her seemed unforgivable.

"*You* didn't kill anyone, Nicole. You'll need to learn to separate from that past life in order to see the bigger picture," Melissa told her.

"But I did, I can see it now, as clear as any memory I have in this life. I killed an innocent little boy. And now this boy is trying to help me, and I can't for the life of me figure out why." Nikki paused and then asked Melissa, "Do you know why? Have you known this whole time that I killed him?"

"Again, you did not kill him. Not the you that is sitting here next to me. I have only recently learned from Ken what happened, and why he is on a mission to save you. And I think that's something you'll want to talk to Ken about yourself," Melissa told Nikki. "He has, quite literally, dedicated his life to helping you.

I'm simply happy that I finally understand Wanda's obsession with you."

Nikki didn't understand and wanted to ask more, but Melissa was pulling her car into the space in front of the shop, and it was time to go inside. From the car, Nikki could see Destiny, sitting in the front window. She seemed to be waiting for them, and Nikki wondered if just living around a shop like this made Destiny a little psychic herself.

Wanda's shop looked different at night, part creepy, part cool and mysterious, and when the bells chimed as they opened the door, Nikki felt like she was home.

Theresa followed them in, also appreciating their surroundings. There was no place quite like a metaphysical shop in the dark to work out the uncertainties of the universe. Within a few minutes of getting there, everyone was visibly settling down. Nikki and Theresa went to each other right away and hugged, Theresa grateful for Nikki coming to her rescue. Rather than go to the back room to debrief, they both felt more comfortable just standing in the shop, surrounded by candles and incense and crystals. Just the sweet scent of whatever was burning in the shop earlier that day worked wonders in calming their nerves.

While they chatted, Melissa lit a candle anointed with rosemary and Road Opener oil before beckoning them to join her in the center of the shop.

Silently, she took Nikki's hand, and then Theresa's, and motioned for them to do the same. They held hands, forming a circle. As soon as they did, Nikki felt a little surge of power run through her, followed by a slight breeze at her back. She closed her eyes and took a deep breath, silently saying hello to Wanda, who she knew was in the room with them. When Nikki opened her eyes, Melissa was looking at her knowingly. She felt Wanda, too.

"From now on," Melissa said, speaking to them softly, "we will watch each other's backs. Somehow you two are now connected psychically, and great care must be taken with your safety."

Theresa now stood up taller, and Nikki thought that she seemed glad to be included.

"Nikki," Melissa continued, "I know that you think you can find James, the person that he *was*, and talk sense into him. I assure you that you cannot. Wanda was right when she told you that you need to forgive, and that is something you should talk to Ken about."

Melissa saw the look on Nikki's face—a mix of embarrassment and uncertainty—and went on without addressing it further. "But right now, we are making a pact to have an open line of communication, to keep each other informed when we are going off in search of answers, and that we will keep the safety of each other in mind when moving forward. Do you both agree?"

"Yes," Nikki and Theresa answered at the same time, which made them smile.

Their circle was broken up by Destiny, who meowed to get their attention. "Hungry?" Melissa asked her and stepped away to fill the bowl.

Nikki followed Melissa into the back room. "So, tell me," she asked, and sat down at the little round table. "Is this the weirdest situation that you've been involved in?"

Intrigued, Theresa sat down next to Nikki, and waited for Melissa's answer.

Melissa presented Destiny with her meal and took a second to think about that question. With the cat purring and happily crunching on her dinner, she shrugged. "I think this is the most dangerous situation that I've been involved with, for sure. But weird? I've had a few of those."

"Care to share one?" Theresa asked, happy for the distraction at that moment.

"A few years ago, before I met Wanda, I got a call from an old friend. Her name was Lizzy. She was eccentric and so much fun, so when she called, I was happy to help. I went to this old farmhouse, where the new owner, a lovely young woman named Annabelle, fell in love with the house's previous owner. They were having a little disagreement that they needed help with."

Nikki rolled her eyes and said, "Oh come on, I think you're forgetting to tell us the punch line. There's nothing weird about a lover's quarrel."

Smiling her mischievous smile, Melissa went on. "Well, there's the little fact that Christian, the previous owner, had been dead for 99 years! They had connected through Annabelle's dreams and fallen in love."

Shaking her head, Nikki said, "Wow, that must have been tough. When your boyfriend is a ghost, what do you do on date night?"

"It was worse than that," Melissa told them. "Christian's ex-fiancé was a powerful wiccan, and she put a spell on him that bound his soul to the earth for 100 years after he had killed himself. Once they fell in love, his time was just about up. He was trying to stay out of Annabelle's life until he left this plane of existence, so that he did not hurt her any longer. She, on the other hand, wanted him to stay."

"Oh my God," Theresa said, and leaned forward on her hands, elbows on the table. "So, what happened?"

"When I left, they had agreed to meet that night. After that, I only heard from Lizzy a few times, but you know what they say. When your times up, it's up." Melissa made eye contact with Nikki, who felt a sort of foreboding in the look she gave her.

They were silent for a moment, and then Nikki spoke up. "So, what do we do next?" she asked.

"I suppose that is up to you," Melissa told her. "I suggest you start by finding Ken and talking to him, and then we will decide what to do about James. Together."

• • • • •

Hadeon stood in the dark outside Wanda's Psychic Powers. He had watched the three women holding hands. "Looks like a bunch of witches inside that shop," he whispered to himself. "And one of them is mine."

He smiled, heart pounding while he watched them. Hadeon did not understand these desires building up in him and he did not care. When he was young and in foster care, adults used to call him words like *blockhead* and *slow*, always making him do physical labor due to his large size, even though he should have been in school. That was nothing compared to what the other kids called him, words like *moron*, *psycho*, and *freak*. From a young age, he struggled not to act on every impulse that he felt, which made his unbalanced nature undesirable for foster care, and eventually landed him a permanent inpatient at whatever institution had a bed available for a state-funded patient.

He knew, even back then, that he was a good person deep down inside, but he struggled to stay good when people were being mean to him. When the internal rage built up, Hadeon didn't know how to control it. And standing there, watching the three women in the shop, his urges were telling him to kill at least one of them.

Something was holding him back, though, a force that he did not understand was preventing him from taking the few steps forward and going inside. He felt, in his body, that the time was not right, so he just stood there, listening to the beat of his heart banging in his ears. With his fists balled, Hadeon smiled again, and waited for the right moment to unleash the wildness that he kept inside.

17
FORGIVENESS

"I am sorry. Please forgive me. Thank you. I love you."

Nikki repeated these words on the bus ride to meet up with Ken. From the Ho'oponopono prayer that he had taught her at her mom's funeral, she felt that no words were more appropriate at the moment.

While Nikki felt safe repeating the words from the prayer, she couldn't imagine asking Ken for forgiveness for real. She knew that in her past life she was so consumed by selfishly being sad about her husband dying that she drank too much and was constantly hungover. She drove to work in the morning many times still drunk from the night before. As a teacher, she had a moral obligation to keep children safe, and she did exactly the opposite of that when she killed little Kenny. She saw the entire accident all over again, from reaching back to stash the bottle to hearing the *clunk* under her tires. Nikki replayed the scene in her mind so many times it was making her feel ill. She also understood her pull toward alcohol and drugs in this life.

If nothing else, she never wanted to use either of those things ever again. *Life lesson number 152*, Nikki thought, *the key to kicking addiction is the cold, hard fact that you can hurt an endless number of people. For infinity.*

As the bus pulled to the stop near their meeting place, Nikki felt nauseous. She was glad that they picked a park—she felt better outside, where she could move around. She saw Ken before the bus doors opened, and for a moment she wanted to sit back down and keep on going. She knew that she would have to face him eventually, though, so she put her head down and went down the steps, the fluttering in her chest getting more serious.

Nikki did not think Ken saw her at first. He had sunglasses on, and was sitting on a swing, looking out at the park. He either did not see her or ignored her, and she hoped it was not because after hearing the details of what she had done to him, he realized he should hate her. She would not blame him.

She walked right up to him and stood directly in front of him, close enough that she could have kissed him, but he sat perfectly still on the swing, the only movement coming from a slight breeze blowing his hair. Nikki wanted to walk away, thinking the worst, when finally, he spoke.

"I have been dreading this day, Nikki," he told her quietly.

Nikki thought that their friendship was over. "I am so sorry, Ken," she said. "I have no excuse for what I did to you. I don't blame you if you hate me. I—" She started to cry, which felt like a lame way of regaining his sympathy, but she could not help it.

Ken removed his sunglasses and she saw that he had been crying, as well. He reached out, took her hand, and said, "I haven't been dreading this day because it would mean the end of our friendship. I have been dreading it because I know the hurt it would cause you. If you were not in danger, I would have protected this truth for lifetimes."

Nikki could not help but ask, "Why don't you hate me?"

Ken squeezed her hand and said simply, "You made a mistake, Nikki. It was a big one with consequences, yes, but a mistake nonetheless. No one should be punished like you have been for one moment in time. You have always been a good person, no matter what your lives have thrown at you, and that counts, too."

"But, Ken, I literally ran you over with my car," Nikki said the words slowly, as if he couldn't possibly understand the implication of what she had done. "I took you away from your mom. You were all she had. That is unforgiveable."

"Yes, and do you know what else you did?" Ken asked, while pushing his feet off the ground to swing slightly. "You prevented me from enduring a life in the foster care system. My mom was sad, sure, but she also didn't know at the time that she was already dying of cancer. Two months after I died, she died, too. We were able to be together again, all of us, me, my mom and dad. The happy life that you think you ruined for me would not have existed. All you did was spare me from the pain of losing my only living parent and a lifetime of suffering."

Nikki almost didn't believe what Ken was saying. She *saved him*? That sounded a little too 90s sitcom ending for her to believe. He could tell by her bewildered expression that she wasn't seeing that what he said was true.

"Even if that's true, I still did a horrible thing," Nikki told him. She sat down on the swing next to Ken and sighed.

"Sure, okay," he said. "You did a bad thing. If I had not been killed, if you had run over an unoccupied bike in the street, would you have punished yourself like you did?" he asked her.

She thought about that for a moment and answered, "No, I guess not. I probably would have freaked out and changed my life. Stopped drinking. Made myself deal with my grief."

"Exactly!" Ken shouted the word, like getting through to Nikki was the greatest moment of his life.

Finally, and slowly, Nikki smiled. A weight she didn't even know she had been carrying was lifted. Not set free but lighter at least.

"Is that why you saved me that day, when you found me in the garbage? Did you know who I was?"

Nikki asked him. She thought back to the day at the NA meeting, when he told her that God brought him here to bring her peace. It wasn't God after all, Nikki realized. It was Ken's mission all along.

Now it was Ken's turn to sigh. "My greatest curse, and blessing, is the gift of memory. At some point in each of my lives, I have recalled vivid details from my past lives. I overheard what you asked of James right after our accident, and I recalled that memory when I was a teenager in this life. I have been looking for you ever since."

"To save me?" Nikki asked, amazed by this person who saved her life once, and was trying to save it again.

"Yes. I do not agree that you need to punish yourself like this. I see the cycle of murder and death and punishment as a downward spiral that you can be stuck in for a very long time. I couldn't let myself be the cause of that," Ken said, and stopped his slow swinging to look her in the eye. "It's not just that I want to save you. I want you to know that I forgive you. And you should forgive yourself."

"Now you sound like Wanda," Nikki told him.

"You've spoken to Wanda?" Ken asked, surprised.

Nikki shrugged her shoulders, trying to look casual as she said, "Yes, we spoke a few weeks ago. Before I did the past life session with Melissa."

"How?" he asked.

"Through Melissa. She's a medium, too, you know. Wait, did you know Wanda?" Nikki asked, realizing the intensely interested look on Ken's face.

Ken smiled and confessed, "Wanda was my great-grandmother. Well, in my last life, that is."

Stunned, Nikki was at a loss for words. She opened her mouth to speak, but instead of speaking, she just stared at Ken, waiting for more.

"After the accident, she was one of the first souls to greet me. I was so upset by what I heard you doom yourself to that I begged her to help me. She agreed to try to find you in this life, and while she was against interfering with your wishes, she would at least try to help you to forgive yourself. Unfortunately, she died before you came into our lives, and so, she decided to stick around and finish out her promise."

"Yes, she was pretty intent on me forgiving myself. Although she wouldn't tell me for what," Nikki said. And then, thinking about how wild this all sounded, she said, "That's so cool. I mean, you had your great-grandma from your past in your present. That must have been fun," Nikki said.

Ken shook his head and explained, "No, it was pretty hard, actually. You see, I have the gift of memories from my past lives, but she did not. Besides me being a customer of hers at the shop, she had no idea who I was until she died." Ken smiled then and went on, "But that, that was a trip, since she had psychic powers in this life, she was able to stick around and find clever ways to talk to me."

Nikki was confused, and asked, "But if she was a psychic, why didn't she know you?"

"Well," Ken told her, "Since she did not feel it was right to interfere, she blocked herself of that knowledge before she reincarnated. So, while a part of her soul was secretly searching for you in this life, her 'human brain' was left out of that process. It actually made her feel a little nutty at times, feeling like she was on the edge of knowing something, but never getting there. Once she passed on and remembered everything, she was annoyed at me but was still so much happier."

Nikki laughed at this. She felt bewildered but cared for. She thought about all the years she felt all alone in the world, thinking that no one would care or even notice if she lived or died, yet there were people who were out here looking for her.

"So," she said, feeling lighter, "You would go and visit your great-grandma, buy some incense or something, knowing that she was on a mission for you but not being able to talk to her about it? That must have been torture!"

Now Ken laughed, too. "Yes, it was pretty torturous. It's not as if I could ask some strange lady who owned this wild store if she found some girl who used to go by Julie," he told her. "Although, if I had, it might have cleared up why she felt drawn to be extra kind to a strange man that came in and out of her shop on occasion, always looking at her longingly. She probably thought I had a crush on her. Actually, I'm pretty sure that Melissa thought that as well, which is why it was so awkward that day at the cemetery."

"Oh my God," Nikki said. "I can't imagine how awkward that was for you." She got off her swing and stood before Ken one more time, growing serious. "Thank you," she told him. "I still feel bad. Like, really, really bad. But I no longer want to crawl into a hole, and die." At that moment, Nikki had a revelation. Without the weight of the heavy guilt she had been carrying, she realized that she saw a better future for herself. "Actually, I want to live. Sort of a weird feeling for me, and pretty scary since I had asked someone to kill me. I feel like my time is up, and I have to find him."

"Not just asked," Ken clarified. "You and your soul mate had made a binding contract. I'm glad that I have found you and that we got this far in your healing journey. But once a contract is made, it is unbreakable. I have no idea how to help you."

Nikki was scared but still felt stronger than she ever had. "I have to try," she told him. "What I asked him to do is also unforgiveable. Maybe, with Melissa's help, I can make him remember. But you do not have to help me. I already hurt you once; I couldn't bear it if you died twice because of me. And if he kills me, well, I literally asked for it."

The look on Ken's face told Nikki that he disagreed, but he did not say anything. Instead, he got off the swing, took her hand, and started walking out of the park.

"Where are we going?" she asked him.

"To get started. I'm not letting you do this alone," Ken told her, squeezing her hand as they left the park. "We are in this together. My entire life has revolved around finding you and keeping you safe. There is no way that I will not be helping you."

Nikki went along with him. She felt relieved, and honored to be so important to another person. It was as if her life was finally coming together, that happiness was just over the horizon. She just had to live long enough to reach it.

18
CAT AND MOUSE

Hadeon felt like a mountain lion, hunting his prey. The adrenaline that he got from stalking Nikki and her friends was almost sexual, and while he desperately wanted the release of the kill, he found himself enjoying the wait. Like a cat stalking a mouse, this was a slow process that required patience and wit.

He had been trying to be good, to fit in with society. Hadeon even got that job and made enough money for a studio apartment within walking distance. Off the streets and out of the shelters, he had been feeling strong, but ever since he slipped up and killed that woman in the prison, Hadeon felt like he was closer to losing control than he liked to feel. He had done some pretty bad things before, but the blood lust that he was feeling was indescribable. He didn't understand it and really, he didn't give it much thought. Hadeon had been preparing for this his entire life.

After watching this odd group of people for a few weeks, Hadeon thought it was time to learn more about them. It was easy, as people were so quick to talk about each other. Only he had to be careful since Nikki—his key target—had seen him that one time when she was leaving the prison. The fact that they also briefly spoke made the memory a delicious one for Hadeon, as it was the spark that lit his desire.

He had known for a while that Nikki was the daughter of the woman he had killed. He was still at the prison when she came charging in. As a matter of fact, he had just washed the rest of the woman's blood from his hands and was leaving the restroom when she was escorted down the private corridor to talk to the warden. They were so close that he could almost taste her tears, and in the moment that she passed him—not even seeing him—he knew without a shadow of a doubt that she was the one that he had been seeking.

Getting information on the other two was easy. All he had to do was talk to the guys in the locker room at the prison to find out that Theresa was single, lived alone, seldom dated and never dated anyone from work, and was a bitch on wheels if you crossed her. Hadeon was cautious about approaching her or getting too close; there was something about her that made him feel uncomfortable.

While he had no desire to kill or hurt her, something about her made him feel off-kilter, so whenever she was around, he stayed in the shadows and silently followed her. He had successfully followed Theresa outside of work several times, and only made the one slip when he followed her into the woods that day. The thought of Theresa going on a hike, all alone, after someone where she worked was brutally murdered made Hadeon think she was either stupid or extremely fearless. He'd meant to follow at a distance, but he couldn't help himself—he was so intrigued that he got closer and closer, until she saw him. When she twisted her ankle, he used that opportunity to sneak away but knew that their brief encounter would spark some kind of movement from the women, which was fine with him. He was enjoying himself immensely.

A few buybacks to the bartender at the Moonshine Pub a few doors down from Wanda's gave Hadeon lots of gossip about Melissa. Apparently, she had moved around quite a bit before meeting Wanda and moving into the apartment above the shop. Rumor had it that she had fallen hard for Wanda but that was never confirmed. She was liked well enough by the locals, even if people thought she was a bit kooky and eccentric, but she was kind, and always made sure that the shop donated to the local charities. Bobby, the bartender, had gone to see her once after his girlfriend went missing, and it took Melissa all of two minutes to break the news to him that she was not missing but had been killed. A hit-and-run accident that no one even knew about. The cops were able to use Melissa's description of the location and find poor Mary covered by weeds in a ditch about ten miles out of town.

Apparently, Mary had decided to run off and hitchhike to New York City with hopes of being discovered on Broadway, but she never made it there. Of course, once her body was found and the story uncovered, authorities were quick to dismiss Melissa's information and said that one of their deputies found the body during a routine traffic stop. What impressed Bobby the most was the fact that even though she was dismissed by the cops and never given any credit for finding his girlfriend, Melissa's only concern was for Bobby, and how he was processing what had happened. She couldn't have cared less about the acknowledgement, which made Bobby and everyone else in town believe that Melissa was the real deal.

No one knew much about Nikki, though. There was a guy sitting at the bar who thought that she used to be a hooker or something, but Bobby thought that was just a nasty rumor started by jealous girlfriends. She never came into the bar, never even peeked in. Curiosity got the best of Hadeon, and he followed her to work one day. He couldn't help it; he had to go inside and talk to her. Blue contact lenses covered the color of his eyes. Hadeon knew that he had a memorable eye color and was used to taking that simple precaution, as he had done on the day that he met Janice. Black was a favorite of his as it generally made people wary and want to keep their distance from him. He pulled a baseball cap down as far as he could to hide as much of his face as possible. Pushing the door open, he entered Wanda's Psychic Powers.

When he walked inside and the bells on the door alerted Nikki that a customer had entered, his heartbeat kicked up a notch. Or several notches. It was almost closing time and getting dark outside, which gave Hadeon a sense of comfort and protection. He always slid into the background better in the dark.

At first look, there was no one there to greet him. Immediately, he was drawn to a large wooden statue in the corner of the room. It looked like a man with several arms and an elephant's head. The details were intricate, and he could only make out a broken tusk in one hand and what looked like a bowl of candy in the other. He went to it, and reached out to touch it, when he jumped back at the sound of a voice.

"That is Ganesh," Nikki told him, slowly appearing from some room in the back of the shop. "Or rather, Lord Ganesha. He is a popular deity that is known to be a remover of obstacles." She started to come around the counter, focused on the statue, when she stopped in her tracks. She seemed to be studying his face, and even though he had the contacts in his eyes and his hat pulled low, Hadeon felt seen. Naked. He didn't know if he should turn and run out the door or pin her down and wring her scrawny neck.

"Have you been in the shop before? You look familiar," she questioned, looking him up and down.

"No, ma'am," he answered, focusing on keeping his voice relaxed. "I'm just here for some..." Hadeon looked around the shop quickly and said the first thing that he could pronounce. "Incense. Birthday gift for my mom."

Seemingly satisfied, Nikki gestured to a whole shelf of choices. "Let me know if you need any help," she told him.

Hadeon looked over the incense. He had never seen so many different kinds. Sticks and cones of every scent. His nose burned as he grabbed a handful of floral-scented sticks and brought them to the register. It looked old-fashioned, with large buttons and no credit card machine in sight.

Nikki noticed him looking at it and told him, "I love this old clunker. It's slow but reliable. Kind of like the staff here," she chuckled.

Without meaning to, Hadeon let out a laugh. It surprised him, as laughter didn't come easy for him. He never did have much of a sense of humor.

He paid with cash, and while he did so, he amused himself by thinking that he earned the cash from the prison where he killed this girl's mother. When Nikki handed him his change, their skin momentarily touched. When it did, a little electrical shock ran between them. She jumped back a tad, exclaiming,

"Ouch! Sorry about that," while wiggling her fingers. "Looks like I need to invest in better dryer sheets."

Instantly, Hadeon thought of laundry, of a huge washing machine, of the woman he shoved in there after breaking her neck with his bare hands. He looked to Nikki's neck, and felt his pulse quicken.

"It happens," he said, and looked toward the door. He wanted to leave, yet his feet wouldn't move. He wondered if she recognized him from the day they briefly spoke at the prison.

Out of nowhere, Destiny appeared on the counter. She sat right in front of Nikki, in between her and Hadeon, and hissed at him.

Nikki gasped and said, "Bad kitty," swiping her off the counter. To Hadeon she said, "I'm so sorry about that. She isn't so friendly."

Hadeon tried to conceal his annoyance. He hated to be started, and told Nikki, "That's okay. It must smell my cat on me."

He didn't have a cat, of course, but it seemed like the easiest explanation. Animals never did like him.

"I'm Nikki, by the way." She surprised him with the introduction.

Taken aback, he said, "Hadeon." *Stupid,* he thought. *Why would you tell her your name?*

"Well, it's nice to meet you, Hadeon," Nikki said, and pushed the register drawer shut.

"Um, you, too," he told her, finally able to turn himself away and toward the exit.

He left without saying goodbye, but Nikki didn't mind. From the back of the store, Melissa and Theresa emerged.

Melissa went to Nikki, whose hands were shaking, and gave her a squeeze. "You did good," she told her. And to Destiny, who was purring loudly on the floor, looking proud of herself, Melissa said, "And good job to you, too, little one," and scratched her on the head.

"Thanks," Nikki said, fighting the sick feeling that was rising from her gut. "You think that's him?"

"I didn't get a good look at him from back there," Melissa told her. "All I have is a description that Bobby gave me after he realized that he spilled way too much information to some stranger the other day."

"Yeah, but you're the psychic. You're the one who knew he was coming." Nikki said, looking Melissa in the eyes. "Is it the guy who killed my mom, or just some weirdo who has a crush on you?"

Melissa started to nod yes when Theresa, who had been looking out the window after he left, interrupted, and told them, "It's him."

"How do you know?" Nikki asked.

"I recognize the voice. That guy works with me. I've really only seen him from a distance, though. What did he say his name was again?"

"Hadeon," Melissa answered for Nikki. "It's an old Ukrainian name. It means destroyer."

Nikki and Theresa both looked at Melissa, and she explained, "Seems I'm really tapped in today."

Now Nikki went to the window near Theresa and peered out. She didn't see him but knew that he must be nearby. Confused, she said, "But his eyes. I was expecting amber. Or black."

"Contacts," Melissa said. "It's the easiest way to change or hide something recognizable about yourself, especially when you've got eyes that people would remember."

"That's funny, I thought that he was using contacts to make his eyes that gold color," Theresa said, remembering back to when he followed her in the woods. "Smart, but still, he's pretty stupid to come in here and talk to you. And he told you his name."

Nikki smiled at her own quick thinking. "I took him by surprise, I think, when I told him my name," she said, feeling a bit sinister. Sinister, brave, and perhaps a tad reckless. "That's not the only surprise in store for Hadeon, though."

"Okay, easy," Melissa said, worried about Nikki's tone of voice. "We need to have a plan before we go rushing into battle."

Nikki smiled and told them that she and Ken were working on that.

"The pact, remember?" Melissa told her. "We should at least know what's happening."

"Well then, let's get started," Nikki said as she marched over to the door, locked it, and swung the sign around to read Closed. Wanda, seemingly unhappy with the way things were going, swirled around the room, knocked over a stack of books about the healing powers of water, and left through the door that Nikki had just locked, wildly jingling the bells as she passed.

19
THE BEST LAID PLANS

It seemed like a decent enough plan. Nikki felt fortunate that Ken was willing to help her. While Melissa and Theresa were becoming great friends who wanted to protect Nikki and keep her alive, they weren't sold on the idea of purposefully tracking down Hadeon and trapping him with Nikki until she could convince him not to kill her.

"Honestly, I'm a little sorry that I shared any of our plans with them. I think that Wanda interferes with their opinions a bit," she told Ken over dinner at their favorite diner. Nikki thought that she'd be too nervous to eat but instead, she was ravenous. "She just wants me to forgive myself so that my soul will be saved. I don't see why I can't do that, and save James from the pain of hurting me," she said, swirling a huge forkful of spaghetti and topping it off with a meatball before popping it into her mouth.

"Because James is Hadeon, with no memory of anything else, that's why," Ken explained, while picking at his grilled cheese sandwich. "I happen to want to save both your soul, your life, and that of your soul mate, but we have to be careful about this. I see Wanda's point. I just don't happen to fully agree."

Grateful, Nikki said, "Okay, so let's go over this plan again."

It was going to be easy. At least that's what they told each other. The plan was for Ken to go into the prison and ask to speak with Hadeon. Hadeon, who presumably didn't know who Ken was, would agree to step outside for a quick word. Nikki would pull up in Ken's car and tell Hadeon to get in or Ken would go inside and tell the guards at the door who killed Janice. When Hadeon got in, Ken would join them and she would then drive the half block to the police station, so he couldn't hurt them, and finally, they could explain everything.

"I'd feel better if we had a Taser or something, just in case," Nikki told Ken after she pushed her empty plate away.

Ken grimaced. "Yes, we should have a hostage in my vehicle, along with a weapon, when we pull into the police station, Nikki."

A nervous laugh escaped from Nikki, but she agreed with him. She knew that she ought to feel vulnerable, but what she felt, above all, was determined.

Against Ken's wishes, Nikki paid the bill before they left. When he tried to insist, she playfully nudged him in the arm and said, "Seriously, Ken? I ran you over with my *car*, for heaven's sake. The least I can do is buy you dinner."

He started to protest, and tell her that it wasn't *her*, really, when he stopped and said, "You know what? You're right." They linked arms, and, nervous but committed to their plan, walked like that out of the diner and into the parking lot.

· · · · ·

From behind a car about twenty yards from where Nikki and Ken left the diner, Hadeon was fuming. Did she have a *boyfriend*? he wondered. A goddamn *boyfriend*?

Hadeon had no idea how to place the ridiculous feeling burning in his chest. He wanted to kill this girl, and yet, seeing her with some guy...he was working himself into a jealous rage. Nikki and this guy were walking straight toward Hadeon. He ducked, hitting the ground with his knees, suddenly afraid of being busted. He wasn't ready to kill her and wanted to find more out about her first, like why was she in his dreams all the time? Why did she incite such blood lust? But most important, he wanted to know who she was with, and why it made him feel so crazed.

Burning acid made its way up Hadeon's chest. He thought that if he opened his mouth, fire would come out. Like a dragon, he would engulf the entire town in flames.

.   .   .   .   .

As Nikki and Ken walked through the parking lot, she stopped to face him. She took his hand in hers and said, "I just wanted to thank you, again. I couldn't do this without you."

They embraced, briefly, and Ken whispered something in her ear. She didn't hear it, though. All Nikki could hear was blood whooshing through her ears, as she stared right into Hadeon's amber eyes.

In a flash, he went from kneeling on the ground behind someone's red Oldsmobile, to lunging at her. Nikki pushed Ken away, thinking that Hadeon was attacking her, but she realized, too late, that he was not going for her, but for Ken. A knife flashed in Hadeon's hand, and it came down, quick, toward Ken, who was falling thanks to Nikki's shove.

The two men hit the ground together, Ken from the fall and Hadeon from throwing his body on top of him like a wolf pouncing on a wounded animal. The knife fell to the asphalt as Ken tried to kick Hadeon off him. Nikki screamed and the commotion began to draw a crowd.

"Hadeon, please, stop!" Nikki pleaded. She thought that he either didn't hear her or didn't care, because he scrambled for the knife even as Ken struggled to fight him off. Ken grabbed at the back of Hadeon's shirt and, swinging around, knife now in hand, Hadeon grabbed a hold of Ken's arm and yanked it off him, smashing it to the ground. Nikki could hear the crunch of bone as Hadeon pushed the force of his weight on the spot. She gasped, and her heart seemingly stopped as Hadeon turned his head, looked her right in the eyes, and smiled. He then seemed to notice the people gawking at them, some coming closer, and as fast as he had lunged at Ken just moments ago he released Ken and was gone.

Unsure if she should chase after Hadeon or tend to Ken, Nikki stood dumbly, frozen in her spot. She tried to follow him with her eyes, but it seemed like he vanished.

"What in the fuck just happened?" It was the first time that Nikki had ever heard Ken curse, and she quickly knelt by his side. He cradled his arm as he sat up with her help.

"That was Hadeon. Or James. Oh, you know what I mean," Nikki told him. "Are you okay? I'm pretty sure I heard your arm break."

"I am most definitely not okay," Ken said, putting his other hand on Nikki's back. "But neither are you. You're shaking."

Nikki looked at her hands and realized that yes, she was shaking. Her entire body was vibrating with adrenaline. She was in shock that Hadeon had attacked Ken and not her, and was thankful that he didn't kill him. "Why did that happen?" she wondered out loud.

"Well," Ken answered, presuming that she was asking him. "You *did* make an agreement with him to make you suffer before he killed you. As he gets closer, he's probably conflicted, deep down somewhere." He tried to stand but couldn't quite get himself off the ground. "You failed to mention that this guy is like 100 percent muscle."

A few of the people who gathered around them went to Ken now, checking him over, asking about calling the police. "No, no, it's okay. I'm fine. Just an angry ex, is all," he explained, trying to avoid the burden of having cops delay their plan even further.

Ken forced himself, with Nikki's help, to get up off the ground and put his signature smile back on. Nikki thought that in another life, Ken would make an excellent politician.

The people dispersed, and Nikki and Ken started the slow walk back toward her apartment. "So much for our terrific plan," she said, shaking her head, still in disbelief.

"Well, you know what they say about the best laid plans," he said, still trying to act casual, but grimacing under his breath.

"No, I actually don't know what 'they' say."

"The best laid plans of mice and men often go awry? Robert Burns?" Ken shook his head as if he was greatly disappointed.

"Okay well, I still don't understand, but I'm a tad sidetracked. Are you sure you're going to be okay? Should we go to the hospital?" Nikki was concerned, and feeling far antsier than Ken seemed.

"I'd rather just figure out what to do next," Ken told her. "I'll stay with you tonight and in the morning we can come up with a new plan."

"You're running the meeting tonight, Ken. Those people need you, too. I'll be fine. Besides, it doesn't look like it's me he's after."

"I don't think that he is exactly being guided by rational thought," Ken said, and then, "Don't you want to come to the meeting?"

Nikki shook her head no. "The last thing on my mind is using, trust me."

Ken walked her home, all the way up the stairs and down the hallway, to make sure that her apartment was safe, and she was locked in for the night. He even checked in the closet, in the shower, and under the bed. Nikki was thankful that her apartment was so small, as there were fewer places to hide.

As she opened the door to let him out, Nikki thought back to the first time she saw the flyer for Wanda's shop. She couldn't believe how much had changed in only a few months, both good and bad.

After Ken left, she sat by the window and watched him leave. She still couldn't believe what she had done in her past life, and how he forgave her like he did. Not only forgave her but dedicated this life to saving her. *Actually*, she thought, *if he's all about saving me, why was it so easy to convince him not to stay tonight?*

Nikki figured that she already knew the answer to that. Ken would somehow find a way to keep her safe throughout the night, and she had no right to stop him. Suddenly exhausted, Nikki crawled into bed, hoping that she would dream up a solution. She had to get Hadeon alone, had to make him remember.

While she slept, Ken looked up an old contact who had left Narcotics Anonymous after a few months and bought a gun.

While she slept, Hadeon stood, barely concealed near the streetlight, and watched her window.

While she slept, the energies of the universe kicked into high gear. An agreement was made, a contract was formed, and that is bound to the soul. It is nearly impossible to change what is written in the light of the stars.

20
HOSTAGE

"Juliet-ta, I've found you," Hadeon whispered through the night. Under the light of the moon, Nikki tried to find a place to hide, but every time she thought she had outrun him, Hadeon was right behind her. After running in what seemed like circles, she thought that maybe she had lost him, and ducked beneath some brush.

She felt something move underneath her, a snake maybe, and fought the urge to scream. Cautiously, she raised her body enough to look under it, and discovered it was only some worms. Gross but not a snake, and Nikki breathed a sigh of relief.

Nikki closed her eyes, just for a moment, and suddenly Hadeon was right behind her.

"Boo," he whispered, and when she spun around, she was only inches from his golden eyes.

Nikki screamed and tried to scramble from the ground when she realized that she was getting tangled in sheets. Panting, she was quickly aware that she was in bed and having a nightmare. "Oh my God," she said, trying to throw the covers off her. The room was in complete darkness. Her arms were stretched above her head and when she tried to move them, they would not budge. Struggling and peering into the darkness, Nikki saw that her arms were tied to the bed, rope running around her wrists and through the headboard.

"What in the ..." Her voice trailed off as her eyes adjusted to the darkness, and she saw Hadeon sitting at the foot of her bed, in her desk chair, eyes glowing in the shadows.

Nikki's breath hitched. "Hadeon?" she questioned, although obviously she knew it was him. "What in the fuck? Untie me."

He chuckled and shook his head. "Awful bossy for someone who is tied up," he said, and chuckled again. The sound was deep, raw, and threatening, and then, "How's your boyfriend?"

"Boyfriend? What? Ken?" Nikki, still confused as to how she wound up tied to her own bed, was trying to control her breathing. *Is this it for me*? she wondered, panicking. She had learned all that she had about her past to prevent this very moment, and it could be too late. How on earth could she explain Ken to someone with a psychotic impulse to kill her? "Ken is my friend, not my boyfriend." She twisted and turned on her back, but all of the fight only made her wrists burn. She didn't get anywhere.

"I don't believe you. But it doesn't matter. I'll enjoy watching him mourn you soon enough," Hadeon said as he stood over Nikki. He bent over so close that she could feel his warm breath. She tried to remind herself that the soul of this person was deeply in love with her, and she did not give up hope. She thought he was going to say something else, but instead, he leaned even closer and sniffed her. *Like a dog*, she remembered from her mom's letter.

Wanting to get him talking until she could find an opening to convince him that he didn't have to kill her, Nikki told him, "I know that you killed my mother."

"That I did." He stopped sniffing and smiled, still too close for comfort. Nikki couldn't look away from his eyes as he said, "A slight miscalculation, but I'm not sorry. It felt good to get my feet wet."

Nikki was surprised and asked, "Get your feet wet? You've never killed anyone before?"

Annoyed, Hadeon stood up and answered, "You know, you're pretty ballsy for a hostage."

"Now I'm a hostage?" Nikki said, trying to goad him into talking more. She figured that she was probably going to die anyway, so what was the harm in pushing back a bit. "I thought you were going to kill me."

"Oh, I am going to kill you," Hadeon told her as he stepped back and started to pace around the room. "I just want to understand something first."

Nikki could feel his fury building. She tried to keep her brave face on as she asked, "And what is that?"

Hadeon went to the foot of the bed and started to lift it, as if he would throw it across the room. He certainly seemed strong enough to do just that. He shook the bed, bouncing Nikki around like a rag doll, wrists straining under the rope, and yelled, "Why do you make me so goddamn angry?!"

Now was the chance, Nikki knew. "I can help you with that, Hadeon. Please untie me and we can talk."

He made a noise that sounded like a laugh but clearly was not. "Not a chance," he told her.

"Okay," Nikki said, "well, can you at least tell me, why me? Why do you want to kill me?" She thought she would start there, lead him into an open discussion about their past together.

Hadeon stared at her for a few moments, as if trying to decide what to tell her. He was silent for so long that she didn't think he would tell her anything. Eventually, he figured if he was going to kill her anyway, why not unburden himself a bit. Besides, he was hoping to get to the bottom of why he felt like a crazy person when he was around her. Wanting to kill was fine with him, it was something that he had always known would happen one way or another, but the feeling of jealous rage confused him. He sat back down in the chair, shook his head as if remembering something awful, and told her one of his earliest memories.

"When I was a little boy, I had a terrible nightmare. I was seven or eight. It was after my mom had died, and I was in a foster home with six other children. Even so, I was all alone. My mother came to me, straight from the grave, dirt all over her body. Her eyes were cloudy, and her voice was dusty as she told me that I had a destiny to fulfill. 'You will never have peace until you do an unthinkable act, Hadeon. You must kill,' she told me. 'Who?' I asked. I begged her to tell me, but she said that I would know her when the time was right. The only guidance that she gave me was that me and this woman had the same birthday."

"June 6," Nikki said, interrupting.

"Yes, and when I asked her more, told her I didn't want to kill anyone, tried to get her to hold me, she shoved me away and fell to the ground. I went to her, but she was dead again. I touched her cheek, and her head rolled to one side, and when that happened her mouth opened, and I could see the worms moving around in there. I was scared and have suffered the same nightmare on my birthday every year. It became my mission to kill this person—you—to make it go away."

He stopped talking, and even in the dark, Nikki could see that his golden eyes were shimmering with emotion. She did this to him, and it made her so sad.

They made brief eye contact and he continued, "As time went on, I thought that it was just a stupid nightmare that didn't mean anything. I tried to forget about it, between birthdays anyway. That is, until I saw you at the prison. It's like you ignited some slow-burning fire in me."

"I am sorry, please forgive me," she told him.

"What the hell are you sorry for? I'm the one who is going to kill you," he said.

"It's from a prayer. I am sorry. Please forgive me. Thank you. I love you."

He laughed and said, "Don't pray. I tried that for years and all it got me was bounced around in foster care, and then the nuthouse until I turned eighteen. Trust me, no one is listening."

Nikki tried to sit up, to go to him, but realized she was still tied up. "It's all my fault, Hadeon. And I am sorry. Now let me tell you my story. Do you believe in reincarnation?" she asked.

"Reincarnation? What? No, I don't believe in anything," he huffed.

"I understand. Neither did I, until I met Ken—he's my sponsor, not my boyfriend—and Melissa and Theresa. And Wanda. Just hear me out and then you can kill me if you want to." Nikki was talking fast, hoping that he would let her get it all out. "You and I are soul mates. We have lived many lives together—some happy, some hard, but always together. In my most recent past life I did something terrible. I had a car accident, and I killed a little boy. I died, too, and when I saw what I had done, I was too devastated to move on. It was my fault. I wanted to drift away and lose my soul. You promised me that in my next life, I would be alone and that I would suffer, and that somehow, you would kill me. We made a binding contract, and I was wrong—I should never have let you do that for me."

Nikki struggled to look at Hadeon, who was still sitting in the chair. He didn't respond, as if he hadn't even heard her, so she continued to talk, knowing this could be her only opportunity. "The little boy is Ken, and he has shown me that accidents do not need to be punished like this, and he has forgiven me. I wanted to find you to stop you from killing me, so that I can save your soul."

Still nothing. She continued, "When you die and move on, and you will remember what you did to me, and you will remember all our many lives together. I'm afraid that you will not be able to forgive yourself and we will end up in the same cycle."

Trying to sit up again, Nikki looked at Hadeon, whose eyes were slits as he stared at her. "Oh, for Christ's sake," she said, tired of being tied up and out of words, "Will you untie me? Will you say *something*?"

In the span of just a second or two, Hadeon was standing over her again, but this time, he was holding the same knife that he attacked Ken with.

"You want me to respond to that bullshit?" He spit the words out at her. "I expected you to beg for your life but don't involve me in your ridiculous fairy tale."

"Seriously?" Nikki asked. "You have tracked me down to kill me and you have killed my mother for no reason, all based on a nightmare? Yet I'm the ridiculous one? You can't see any truth to what I'm saying? Maybe the reason you attacked Ken with zero provocation is because you were jealous?" She knew that she was goading him but didn't care. Her breathing was labored, and she felt like she had just been in a physical fight. She didn't know how much more adrenaline her body could take.

"I-I think I'm going into shock," she told Hadeon, who had taken just one step back. "I'm freezing. Do you feel that?" Nikki thought she was losing her mind as the wind kicked up in her room.

She barely heard Hadeon when he said, "Enough talking. It's time to end this."

Looking around she saw that her windows were still shut, and just as Hadeon raised his knife, a force knocked him back against the wall. The knife went flying from his hand. He tried to get up, but the wind kept him on the floor, scrambling for his weapon but unable to reach it.

Relief flooded through Nikki's entire body as she realized what was happening.

In less than a minute, the wind stopped, and Hadeon, panting, got up from the ground. Cautiously he looked around the room, and said to Nikki, "What in the fuck just happened?"

He realized then that she was smiling, and she said, "Oh, that was Wanda."

"What?" he asked, but before Nikki could answer him, the door to her apartment flew open and in walked Melissa, followed by Ken, who was pointing a gun right at Hadeon's chest.

"I see you've invited some guests to our little party," Hadeon said to Nikki, seemingly unfazed. "And how on earth did you know that we would be chatting here tonight?" he asked Melissa and Ken.

Hadeon didn't seem the least bit concerned that Ken had a gun, but he had clearly been surprised by Wanda's turbulent interference.

Melissa responded calmly, telling him, "There is someone that has been beating down my door to talk to you. I think it's time you listened."

Hadeon just stared at Melissa, while he did not speak, his face was pretty clear that he was not interested in what she had to say.

Nikki asked, "Wanda wants to speak to him?"

Melissa shook her head no, and Ken moved closer to Hadeon, still pointing a gun directly at his chest. "Not Wanda. It's Deidra, Hadeon's mother."

21
MAMA

It turned out that the gun came in useful, because it was the only way that Ken and Melissa got Hadeon to sit down. It took them a good twenty minutes to force him back into the chair, while Nikki sat on the edge of the bed, rubbing her wrists and staring at Ken with awe.

She couldn't believe that he, a God-fearing do-gooder, was pointing a gun at someone, forcing them into submission. She thought it was the most incredible act of kindness she had ever seen, in a weird and totally messed-up sort of way. To make matters even more complicated, his left arm was in a sling; it was clearly wrapped by someone other than a medical professional, but it kept him from moving it and creating more of an injury. It also meant that he had to hold the gun still one-handed, which was no easy feat.

Finally, Hadeon settled, seeing that he had no choice in the matter. He told himself that he did not believe anything that Nikki had told him, but he was exhausted and losing the stamina needed to keep on fighting. Besides, Ken was pointing a gun at his chest, and he seemed like the kind of guy who didn't exactly know much about gun safety. He also figured that if he relaxed a bit, so would Ken, and he was bound to put the gun down at some point, especially considering his injury.

Melissa saw Hadeon start to relax into the chair and took the opportunity to connect with him. She had been sitting next to Nikki on the bed, and she whispered to her, "His mother has been hounding me for hours. I've got to do this so she can move on from here."

For some reason, the image of a spirit following Melissa around, annoying her, was amusing, and she stifled a laugh. She watched as Melissa sat on the foot of the bed, opposite to Hadeon. To Ken she said, "Do you really need to keep that thing pointed at him?"

"Sorry, I left my duct tape and rope at home," he quipped to her and then said, "There is no way he will sit here long enough for you to connect with his mother if he isn't forced to." To Hadeon he asked, "Am I correct?"

Hadeon's answer was gruff but honest. "Yup, the man speaks the truth," he said.

Remembering what Bobby at the bar had told him about Melissa, Hadeon was feeling nervous. He wouldn't show it to these *intruders*, but he was both hopeful and terrified to think that his mother was still around. Besides the yearly nightmare, he never had any indication that his mom was a spirit around him, or that she wanted to talk to him. Had she been looking out for him, he wondered. And if so, was she disappointed that he had not yet killed Nikki? Worse, he had killed the wrong woman. Even more terrible, he had enjoyed himself.

Hadeon felt eager enough that he did not fight Melissa when she reached out and took his hands in her own. "I feel like we are a little past the part where I explain to you what is happening and what to expect when I channel your mother. We're going to just jump in with both feet here, Hadeon," she told him. "But I'm right here for you, if you have had enough, just tap me here"—she tapped her left knee—"and I'll make sure that we wrap it up quickly."

Nikki was impressed by how warm Melissa could be, even after bursting into the room to find him about to kill her.

Hadeon's mother was so eager to talk through Melissa that Melissa was practically thrown from the end of the bed when she entered her consciousness.

"Hadeon? Oh my heaven and stars, it really is you." Boisterous, Deidra spoke through Melissa as if it were the most natural thing in the world. "I have missed you so much, son."

Hadeon froze. He did not speak, telling himself to be careful, that Melissa could be faking.

"It's me, Hadeon," Deidra told him through Melissa's voice. "It's Mama."

"Mama," Hadeon said, flatly, as if he did not believe her at all. "You're my mama, talking to me here through this lady? I have seen some pretty crazy shit, but this tops it."

"*Slidkuite za rotom*! Hadeon, please," Deidra spoke in Ukrainian, the language of her home country, what she spoke as a little girl.

Hadeon only remembered a few phrases from his childhood, and the Ukrainian version of *watch your mouth* was one of them. He looked to Nikki and asked, "Any chance your friend here speaks Ukrainian?"

"Nope," Nikki answered, hopeful that he believed her. "Not only does she not speak Ukrainian, but she couldn't fake an accent to save her life."

He looked at Melissa again, this time leaning forward in his chair, with much more interest. "Mama?" he asked, "It's really you?"

"Yes, my dear, dear boy. I have been seeking a way to reach you for what seems like an eternity."

"But Mama, you speak to me every year, on my birthday. I'm sorry to say I've come to dread those talks, Mama. You scare me." Hadeon both felt and sounded like a little boy.

Tears fell from Melissa's eyes as Deidra spoke. "Oh sweetheart, that is what I have been desperately trying to tell you. Those dreams...those nightmares...they are not me. They are a manifestation of a piece of your inner consciousness.

You have been using my image to convince yourself to do something terrible."

Hadeon sat up straight. He rubbed his face, shook his head no. "Was not you?" he asked, slowly.

The voice that came from Melissa was so sorrowful, it was heartbreaking. "No, my dear. It was not me but you. I am so sorry."

Hadeon reached out and took Melissa's hand. "Oh Mama," he said, tears flowing down his cheeks and landing on their hands. "Oh Mama, it is I who am sorry. I did something terrible. I hurt someone. I thought...I thought that you told me to do it."

"No, son, but listen to me. What this girl here tells you is the truth," Melissa's head turned, and her eyes landed on Nikki. "You promised that she would suffer, and you promised that you would end her life. I'd like to tell you that your soul is strong enough to break that agreement, but your fate is now in your hands."

Hadeon could see that his mother's presence in Melissa was fading. Her eyes were clearing, and the tears had stopped. "Please, don't go," he told her.

"I'd love to say that I can stay and help you, but I have waited a long time to move on. I love you, son." Melissa lifted her hand to wipe her tears, and by the time she brought her hand back down, Hadeon could tell that his mother was gone.

22
NOT THIS TIME

When Nikki's birthday rolled around about a month later, it wasn't lost on her that it was also Hadeon's birthday. He was out there somewhere, although she hadn't seen him since the night that his mother used Melissa to speak to him.

After his mom had gone, Hadeon simply sat there, in stunned silence, tears rolling down his face. Ken had long since put the gun down, and Melissa had disappeared into the bathroom; she told them later that she had absorbed so much emotion from Deidra that she cried on the floor for close to an hour before she was able to recover enough to rejoin them. By the time she did, Hadeon had left.

Nikki told her that he just got up, shook Ken's good hand, and walked out of the room. A few seconds later, he came back and said to Nikki, "I'm really sorry for what I did to your mom. I have no idea what to do now," and he left.

Melissa filled Nikki and Ken in on the details about how Hadeon's mother found her, that she had been so frantic for a way to reach her son that she begged Melissa to channel her. Deidra confessed that while she had always wanted a baby, was even desperate for one as her hormones were changing after marriage, she knew that she should not have had a child with Hadeon's father.

"Apparently, he was a mean bastard," Melissa told them. "After a while, Deidra realized he was a psychopath, and she was glad that he left them. When Hadeon was a baby, he was so good that he hardly made a peep. But at times, Deidra felt like she was suffocating, that she was doomed to a lifetime with this child of hers. There was no reason for her to feel that way, and it was only after she died of a sudden illness that she learned that Hadeon was born to kill. His very name meant 'destroyer,' and he would live up to it." The thought of what she had done to him made Nikki want to shrink into herself and die. His mom was just another check in the box of people's lives that she ruined.

"Honestly, I was surprised when Deidra's spirit found me," Melissa confided. "I've been feeling a bit off lately, like I was losing some of my abilities or something. But she came blowing into the shop like a tornado. She told me that she had been giving him signs for the past twenty years or so, but he was stubborn—and sad, I guess—and he never picked up on them."

Ken gave Melissa a little pat and told her that constantly worrying about another person's safety is exhausting, to which Melissa nodded in agreement.

Ken then stepped outside to call Theresa, who was upset that she had missed saving Nikki and watching the scene with Hadeon and his mom unfold. After that, she slowly left the little circle that they had formed. It seemed that without the impending danger, they didn't have much in common. They hadn't even sensed Wanda around. Nikki thought that maybe she moved on, now that she was safe, but Melissa insisted that she still felt the energy of her spirit around her.

On Nikki's birthday, Ken and Melissa had a little party for her at Wanda's. It was just them and a few customers who Nikki had grown fond of. They got her a cake and some flowers, and put a little birthday hat on Destiny, who immensely enjoyed the dish of sardines that Melissa put down for her when the cake was brought out. When they sang "Happy Birthday" and told her to make a wish, all she could think of was Hadeon, and wished that he had found peace.

It was her twenty-sixth birthday. Even though Nikki was free from danger and was no longer worried for her safety, she withdrew a bit, sticking to the shop and the occasional meeting with Ken. She was glad that Hadeon no longer wanted to kill her, but she felt so sad for putting him in that position, not to mention getting her mom killed because of it, that she had a hard time sleeping at night. She had no idea where he was, or if he was okay, or how he was dealing with everything.

After the cake was finished and Nikki said goodbye to her friends, she was ready to spend some time alone. Declining Ken's offer to walk her back to her apartment, Nikki gave Destiny a good snuggle before she kissed the top of her head, and set out on her own. Although it was dark and she had at least a ten-minute walk, she felt no fear as she put her face up to the breeze and smiled. "Happy birthday," she told herself.

From a few feet behind her, Nikki heard what was unmistakably Hadeon's voice, say to her, "Happy birthday to you, Nikki."

Nikki whipped around to find Hadeon's bright amber eyes staring at her from under a baseball hat. She smiled; she couldn't help herself. "Hadeon," she said. "Happy birthday." She didn't know how to approach him, so she stayed where she was.

"Shouldn't you be afraid of me?" he asked her.

"No way. Not now that you know the truth. I've been worried about you," she told him, daring to take one step closer. "I want you to know that you don't have to feel any guilt. This is all my fault, and..."

"Nikki, I killed your mother. What do you think, we are going to pick up where we left off in some past life, and be together?"

Nikki could tell that he was angry, and she stopped in her tracks. "No, I mean, I guess not," she said, feeling dejected. She knew that the man in front of her was her soul mate but saw then that he didn't want to be with her. She realized that she had been creating a fantasy in her mind where they would end up together. She felt ridiculous.

"So then, why are you here?" she asked him.

"I wanted to tell you that I've done some soul-searching," he said. "A lot of soul-searching, in fact. I even did a past life regression with a hypnotist Upstate who specializes in past lives, and I remembered everything. I-I wanted to tell you that it is not all your fault. I wanted you to join me again so badly that I did not give you the time and space to heal. We are both responsible, Nikki, not just you."

Tears rolled down Nikki's face, even though she didn't realize she had started to cry. "Really?" she asked him, while she took tentative steps to bridge the gap between them. Her birthday flowers slid from her hand and hit the ground as she reached out for him.

"No," Hadeon said, holding his hand up to stop her. "Please, don't come any closer. I couldn't bear it. I do remember, but that does not change what I have done. The person that I became in order to hurt you, to hurt your mom, is not someone who I want you to be around. I'm not someone who *I* want to be around."

Deflated, Nikki told him, "I am so, so sorry."

A sad smile formed on Hadeon's lips. "I forgive you, it's myself that I'm still working on."

Nikki nodded at that. She understood, but she still wanted more. She had overcome so much in this life—her dad dying, her mom in prison, drugs, prostitution, recovery—she wondered what the benefit of breaking the cycle is if there is no happiness after. "Well, thanks for not wanting to kill me anymore," she said, trying to lighten the moment a bit.

It worked. Hadeon smiled and told her, "If Ken could forgive you and spend his life trying to save you, and you found it within yourself to forgive your past self, who am I to take all that away?"

"You're my soul mate," she said pointedly. "You really are here for me. I want to be here for you now, too."

Hadeon still would not close the distance between them. "I have to find a way to recover from all of this, Nikki. I truly don't know who I am right now. I've lived my whole life thinking that my dead mom sent me on a mission to kill you. I need some space. Like, a lifetime of space, to figure this out."

"So, I guess we have to figure out how to have separate lives this time around?" she asked.

"It looks like it, Jules," he said, using her name from their past life. It gave her chills, and then, surprising both of them, Hadeon took the last few steps between them and embraced Nikki, squeezing the last bits of stress and worry right out of her.

"I know it's crazy, but I still want to be with you," she told him. She was hanging on for her life, not wanting to let go.

Hadeon whispered back, "Not this time, my love. Not this time."

23
TWIN FLAME

After Nikki had left the shop and the few guests left, Melissa and Ken quickly cleaned up, working together comfortably.

"You know, it is kind of odd that Theresa has just disappeared from Nikki's life, don't you think?" Melissa asked Ken as she dumped the dirty cake plates into the trash. "She couldn't even show up to her birthday celebration?"

Ken, who had gotten his arm professionally set and cast, shrugged his shoulders, and said, "Who knows. It kind of seemed to me that she was developing a little crush on Nikki, maybe she was just trying to be involved in all of this to get closer to her. Now that Hadeon no longer seems to be a threat, they really don't have anything in common at all."

"I guess so," Melissa said, tying up the trash bag. "Hey, are you all right? I know that this has all been pretty difficult for you also. You're a good friend."

"I'm good, thanks. Just trying to figure out where to go from here."

"I hear ya. I do kind of miss Wanda lurking around," Melissa giggled. "It seems like her job may be done, as well. I wish she would have said goodbye, though."

Ken nodded in agreement, and said, "Tell me about it. For being such an overprotective soul, you would think that she'd never leave."

Melissa smiled. She started to ask Ken another question, but he interrupted, looking at his watch.

"Well, I had better get going, as well. Thanks again," he said, and walked out the door, bells clanking as he shut it behind him.

Melissa leaned against the counter by the cash register, and said to herself, "That was abrupt," wondering why had Ken left so quickly. The little tinkle of Destiny's collar got her attention, and she watched the cat run to the window, as if she was just as confused as Melissa was as to why Ken left like that. Melissa thought about what he said, about Wanda being an overprotective soul; a weird thing to say about a soul that was once his great-grandmother, someone Ken didn't even know in his last life. His mom, she knew, had been protective, but...something wasn't sitting right. Not really thinking about her actions, Melissa quickly pushed herself off the counter and rushed out the door.

Following Ken was easy, as he stood pretty tall and had a distinct walk. He stood straight and walked quickly, always. Now, he was headed in the direction of Nikki's apartment but suddenly took a left, into an alley that was a dead end. Melissa stood in the shadows of the road split. Straight ahead, down the road a bit, she saw Nikki and Hadeon. It looked like they were having a deep conversation.

Good for them, she thought, so badly wanting for both of them to be happy.

To her left, where the alley ended with a cluster of dumpsters, Melissa saw Theresa step out from behind one, and Ken walked up to her. Clearly, they had planned to meet there.

Melissa wanted to feel embarrassed about following them, wanted to assume they were involved romantically and didn't want anyone to find out, but she knew better. Her psychic abilities may have been lacking lately—she felt very strongly that she was being blocked by something more powerful than her. She had started to feel like she was being guided like a puppet, but she was feeling stronger since things had settled down with Nikki and Hadeon, and she knew that something was off with Ken.

That feeling was confirmed when she saw Ken hand Theresa the gun that he had somehow acquired right before finding Hadeon at Nikki's place.

Creeping closer, pressing herself against the dirty wall of the building that led down the alley, Melissa thought that her heart might beat itself right out of her chest. Now within earshot, she heard Ken say, "You know what to do," before he turned and walked away. He walked so close to Melissa that she had no idea how he didn't see her. She held her breath and stood perfectly still as she watched him walk down the alley and make a left, heading toward where Nikki and Hadeon were.

Theresa just stood there, next to the dumpster, and stared at the gun in her hands. She looked uncomfortable and nervous. Her eyes were wide, and her aura was bright yellow, glowing around her, pulsing. Melissa knew that meant that Theresa was having a serious inner conflict going on, but she didn't have to read her aura to know that, as Theresa looked as if she were afraid to move an inch.

Just as Melissa thought Theresa might chuck the gun in the dumpster and run, she positioned it correctly in her hand. She pointed it in front of her, into the dark street, and slowly placed her finger on the trigger.

"Whoa," Melissa said, which was a mistake because Theresa jumped so much that she easily could have pulled the trigger and killed her.

Melissa stepped out of the shadows and said, "It's okay, Theresa, it's me."

Surprisingly, Theresa pointed the gun at Melissa and said, "You are going to want to walk away from this, Melissa. You are not supposed to get hurt here."

"Let's just put the gun down, okay? And then you can tell me what's going on." Melissa was terrified but could sense that Theresa didn't want to hurt her.

Theresa did not put the gun down, but Melissa continued to walk closer to her anyway. "I can see that you're conflicted," Melissa told her. "I want to help you. Why don't you tell me what's going on, and I can help you work through it."

They were standing face-to-face. Theresa blinked, confused. "Work through it?" she asked. "There is nothing to work through. I need to kill Nikki. I need to. I—"

As Theresa spoke, Melissa looked into her eyes. In each pupil, she saw a glow, a tiny flame.

"Oh my God," she said, interrupting Theresa's rant. "You are his twin flame."

Theresa blinked again, and this time, started shaking her head. Back and forth, "No. No, I didn't mean that. I don't know what I'm saying." She looked up at Melissa, eyes pleading. "I think I'm losing my mind."

Slowly, Melissa reached out and took the gun from Theresa's hand. Theresa let her, and Melissa placed it on the dumpster behind them. Feeling safer, she took both of Theresa's hands in her own and told her, "Sweetie, you're not losing it. When Nikki's soul mate agreed to kill her, he must have known that he wouldn't be able to go through with it. His soul split; half reincarnating as Hadeon, and half as you. You're the backup plan—to kill Nikki if Hadeon could not."

Now Theresa looked at Melissa as if she was the crazy one. "I'm a *backup* plan? That's the entire purpose of my freaking life?"

"Yes, and also no. You are an individual, with your own thoughts and feelings. And free will—you can't forget free will. But yes, you share a soul with someone who loved his soul mate enough to dedicate this lifetime to helping her repent. You are also Nikki's soul mate. You always have been. That's probably why the two of you became friends so quickly. And why you were the one to receive the letter from her mom."

"Oh. Oh wow," Theresa said. "I thought that maybe I was falling for her. And then, I started having these terrible nightmares where I was hunting her down."

Theresa began to shake, her hands trembling in Melissa's.

Melissa embraced her and promised to help get her through this. "Hadeon already broke his end of the agreement. He knows that Nikki forgives herself. You don't have to do this. And Ken forgave her, too." Melissa had been so focused on getting the gun away from Theresa, and then the shock of realizing that Hadeon was not the only soul who was programmed to kill Nikki, that she forgot about Ken.

"Wait," Melissa said, and grabbed Theresa's shoulders. "What does Ken have to do with this?"

"I think he hypnotized me or something," Theresa told her. "He kept telling me that I must kill Nikki. The way it happened made so much sense, I couldn't see any other truth. But now, nothing makes sense."

"Why on earth would he tell you to kill her?" Melissa was so confused, she thought she would lose her mind.

Theresa tried to answer her, but the wind kicked up in the alley. "Wanda?" Melissa felt instant relief, replaced by a fear that she couldn't place. "We need some help here, Wanda!" Melissa had to holler over the wind that whipped between them.

In shock, Theresa fell to her knees. As she did, she was knocked back by an invisible force, her head hitting the side of the dumpster. Blood instantly sprang from her skull, and as Melissa tried to go to her, a pair of hands from behind her pushed her down.

On the pavement now, Melissa turned onto her back, just in time to see Ken grab the gun off the dumpster and aim it directly at her chest.

24
A BLIP IN TIME

"Back off, Melissa." Ken was still pointing the gun at Melissa, and as the wind settled, so did the beating of Theresa's heart. Melissa could see her spirit leave her body, up through her throat and out of the top of her head, in a sliver of white. It hovered over them for a moment, and in a flash, it was gone.

Ken shook his head and laughed. "What a weak one," he said.

He sounded different, less like someone who dedicated his life to helping others and more like someone who had grown tired of pretending to be good.

Melissa wanted to be by Theresa's side, to let her know that she wasn't all alone, but she couldn't move with the gun pointed at her. "You killed her," she yelled at Ken, but he just laughed.

"Me?" he said, feigning surprise. "I didn't touch her."

"Ken, please, don't do this. What happened to forgiveness?" Melissa asked, watching the color of his aura change from green to black. This change, she knew, revealed his true nature. She also knew that it must have been exhausting work to not only change who you appeared to be, but to make the energy that you presented the world match that lie.

She knew the truth before he even spoke, but she let him confess anyway. She didn't have much of a choice.

"Forgiveness?" he said, mockingly. "Oh please. It's all about revenge, baby. Julietta Viola was nothing but a pathetic lush, who ran me over without hesitation. She hit me so hard that she knocked out of my goddamn shoe!" Ken was yelling now, clearly furious. "My brand-new Keds ruined!"

"It was an accident, Ken. You know it was. You said yourself that you would have ended up in foster care."

Again, Ken laughed right at her. "You girls will believe anything," he said. "It's true that my mom would have died of cancer, but she suffered all alone, with no husband and a dead child. She died of cancer, sure, but she really died of a broken heart. And foster care? Not exactly. I would have had a great life with my grandmother. Oh, who also died of a broken heart, literally. She had a heart attack and died right after my mother did."

Melissa just stared at him, speechless. "So, is Wanda your grandma, then?" she asked, bewildered.

She wondered why he wouldn't just tell them she was his grandmother in his past life. Why keep extending the lie?

Melissa tried to stand but the wind came back down the alley and kept her down.

Ken stood up straight and put his kind, formal face on. "Melissa, I'd like for you to meet my mother. Mom," he said, gesturing to nothing in particular, "you already know Melissa." The wind all around Melissa turned even colder, as if Wanda was finally showing her who she really was. Melissa thought back to all the memories she had of Wanda, how she thought that she was her friend and mentor. If she wasn't so scared and worried for Nikki, her heart would have broken right then and there.

Melissa felt disgusted with both of them, while all the truths that she had not seen flooded her head. "Why do all of this for Nikki, then, if you just wanted to kill her? Why make her forgive herself? Why set her up for such failure?" Melissa asked the questions, but as soon as she did, she already knew the answers. Ken didn't just want to kill Nikki, he wanted to crush her. He wanted to build her up just to break her back down. Finding her in the dumpster and killing her then wouldn't have been enough for him.

"Were you even an addict?" Melissa asked him, thinking about the other people he helped, and how he was faking all of it.

Ken smiled and told her, "I sure was." He looked proud of himself and explained, "I had to put myself in alignment with Nikki, or else my plan wouldn't have worked. I did drugs, I became scrawny and weak, and even had the physical withdrawal when I gave them up, knowing time was ticking and I had to set up the perfect stage for my meeting her. I had to save her and to play the part, I put my body through some disgusting things. But don't worry about me, I knew what I was doing all along. My body may have suffered but my mind was perfectly clear."

Melissa knew then that Ken was completely obsessed, and there was nothing that could stop him.

"Now Mom," Ken said to the air around him, "if you'd be so kind as to watch over your business partner and keep her from doing anything stupid, I've got some business of my own to attend to."

While Melissa watched Ken walk down the alley, she struggled to get up. She knew that he was headed right for Hadeon and Nikki, and she had no way to stop him. The harder she fought, the more the wind fought her back. Dust was in her eyes and her teeth. She curled herself into a ball, trying not to suffocate, when she heard the gunshot.

As soon as she did, the wind ceased. Melissa got up and ran for the sound, but it was too late.

•   •   •   •   •

It all happened in seconds, tiny moments that Hadeon could not even track. He saw Nikki, so close to him that he could smell her shampoo. He had never held another person before. If felt, to him, as if a thousand years of stress left his shoulders.

He had his eyes closed, breathing in the scent of her, not wanting to say goodbye but knowing that there was too much hurt between them to ever have a relationship. Hadeon kept telling himself that they would be together in their next life, and it made their parting a small bit gentler.

He was just about to tell her that it was time for them to say goodbye when he heard a loud crack from behind him. Before his brain could catch up to form the thought *gun* the bullet ripped through his back, exited his chest, entered Nikki's chest, and lodged in her left lung.

They fell, still holding each other.

Nikki's body tightened, then convulsed, then relaxed as the bullet settled inside her. Passed out, still in Hadeon's arms, Nikki bled out onto the street. Her blood mixed with Hadeon's, rushing together like long-lost lovers.

As Nikki lay dying, Ken appeared in her fading vision. She smiled at first, thinking he had come to help her, but then she saw the gun. Her quickening pulse sped up the blood loss, but she didn't care. It had been Ken all along, she saw that now, and the truth of that sank into her dying body.

Ken, her savior, pulled her out of a wrecked life just so he could give her hope before shoving her back down. In a way, she got what she wanted.

As Ken turned to leave, she whispered something to him. He couldn't hear her, and so he knelt down, intrigued by what her last words would be. He rolled his eyes as he heard them, so sick of her saying "I'm sorry" that he could scream.

Ken stood and looked at the pair of them on the street. "Oh please," he said to Nikki, giving her body a little shove with his foot. "Just die already. You are exhausting."

Voice a tiny bit stronger this time, Nikki asked one last question, something she had always wondered. "After you died, what did you whisper to your mom?"

"I told her that I'd make you pay," he said.

Nikki nodded and closed her eyes for the last time.

Both Nikki and Hadeon took their final and shallow breaths at almost the same time. Ken smiled, thinking that everything really had worked out as planned. Hadeon turning into a jealous teenager was the only part of this adventure that had really shocked Ken, and besides his broken arm, the situation had been entirely amusing. As he disappeared into the darkness, he picked up a shopping bag that he had stashed on the side of the road before Nikki's party. He slung it over his shoulder and whistled, knowing that his brand-new blue Keds were safe and sound at last. He looked down at his cast, at the spot Nikki had drawn a little heart around her name, and laughed. As Hadeon and Nikki lay dying, Ken began to whistle, and disappeared.

Neither of them heard Melissa, yelling for help, running toward them. As she neared, she knew both Nikki and Hadeon had been shot and killed. She could see both of their spirits exit from the top of their heads, at the crown chakra, at the same time. They combined, circling one another, turning from white to pink and back to white before blinking out of Melissa's vision.

Tears flowed freely down Melissa's face as she heard sirens approaching. She couldn't imagine the story that the cops would tell each other about Hadeon, Nikki, and Theresa. She was sure they would dream up some love triangle tale about them and how one of them must have killed Janice in a fit of rage. It didn't matter, Melissa thought, as she said a final goodbye to her friends. It didn't matter at all. "Just a blip in time," she whispered, wiping her face. "At least now they can be together again."

Melissa stood up as she heard footsteps approaching and took one last look at Nikki, and noticed a small, peaceful smile on her lips. Nikki's last day as Nicole Ingles started on her twenty-sixth birthday, and for her, it was about as happy as she could have hoped for.

The front window at Wanda's Psychic Powers was almost out of eyesight from where Nikki and Hadeon's bodies lay, but Destiny had enhanced vision, even for a cat. She sat by the window and watched everything that happened. When the gun went off, it hurt her ears, but she stayed where she was, to make sure that Nikki's spirit left with Hadeon's.

When it was all over and Melissa got back from being questioned by the police, Destiny jumped into her arms as soon as she walked in the door. Melissa held her and cried, petting her soft fur, calmed by the purr.

Nikki had been on to something when she asked Melissa if Destiny comforted all of her clients as she comforted her. Not all of them, no. But some. The ones that she was sent to watch over. The ones she was sent to love.

∙ ∙ ∙ ∙ ∙

"I know I am deathless...
We have thus far exhausted trillions of winters and summers, There are trillions ahead, and trillions ahead of them."
–Walt Whitman

ABOUT THE AUTHOR

Amy Sampson-Cutler, author of *A Shadow of Love*, is a writer who earned her master's degree in creative writing from Goddard College. Her work can be found in *Slut Vomit: An Anthology of Sex Work*, *Tales to Terrify*, wow-women on writing, the Pitkin Review and more.

She is the Executive Manager at Mount Peter Ski Area, where she grew up skiing in the winter and dreaming up stories in the summer. Her favorite days are spent knocking around story ideas with her husband. She lives in the Hudson Valley with her husband, son, and a ridiculous amount of furry family members.

She can be contacted through AmysHippieHut.com.

Other Titles by Amy S. Cutler

"A spooky love story that gets your heart racing and your spine tingling! For those fans of *The Ghost and Mrs. Muir* who always wanted more, look no further."
–Alexandra Angeloch, playwright

A Shadow of Love

Amy S. Cutler

Note from Amy S. Cutler

Word-of-mouth is crucial for any author to succeed. If you enjoyed *To Have and to Hold, to Love and to Kill: An Agreement of Souls*, please leave a review online—anywhere you are able. Even if it's just a sentence or two. It would make all the difference and would be very much appreciated.

Thanks!
Amy S. Cutler

We hope you enjoyed reading this title from:

www.blackrosewriting.com

Subscribe to our mailing list – *The Rosevine* – and receive
FREE books, daily deals, and stay current with news about
upcoming releases and our hottest authors.
Scan the QR code below to sign up.

Already a subscriber? Please accept a sincere thank you for
being a fan of Black Rose Writing authors.

View other Black Rose Writing titles at
www.blackrosewriting.com/books and use promo
code
PRINT to receive a **20% discount** when purchasing.